# Max was sitting in her chair, eyes glued to her computer screen.

*Ohhhhhhhh…*

Not much of a thought, but all she could manage initially.

She reminded herself that she had turned everything off—the flash drive was in her drawer, the printed pages were shoved in her briefcase, and there was no way he could be looking at *Passion Flower*. He was probably looking for the Queensland report, to make some changes.

*So breathe. Breathe and be normal.*

'Mr Rutherford? Is there something you wanted urgently? You should have called me,' she said, forcing herself not to run to her desk but to take it slowly, calmly.

Max raised his head and looked at her— slack-jawed, marvelling, astounded.

And Catherine knew.

Max's voice, when it finally came, was unbelievably husky. 'You wrote this?'

**Dear Reader,**

I'm a Scorpio, so I've always loved the idea of the phoenix—rising from the ashes of an old life to claim a new one. And that's the idea at the heart of TURNING THE GOOD GIRL BAD.

In this case we're taking one prim and proper personal assistant—who is really a wild child in hiding—mixing her with one tough-talking boss with a secret Sir Galahad complex, and getting...

Well, Catherine North and Max Rutherford aren't exactly sure.

All they know is that they have a brilliantly unconventional working relationship that shouldn't be messed with. But when Max accidentally uncovers Catherine's alter ego *messy* doesn't begin to describe the situation.

Catherine suddenly decides it's time to burst out of the cage she's built for herself—but she can't find the key. She thinks Max just might have one that fits, so all she has to do is tell him to open the door. Simple, right?

*Wrong!* Nobody tells Max Rutherford what to do. Oh, he'll fit the key in the lock, all right—but he won't turn it until he's sure Catherine is ready.

And so starts a steamy high-stakes game of seduction, played by two sets of rules but with only one prize—if only they can agree on when and how to claim the spoils.

TURNING THE GOOD GIRL BAD is a story about coming to terms with who you are and what made you that way. It's about rising from the ashes, showing off your coloured feathers and fighting for the life—and the love—you deserve.

I hope you enjoy watching Max and Catherine turn themselves inside out along the way.

*Avril Tremayne*

# TURNING THE GOOD GIRL BAD

BY
AVRIL TREMAYNE

MILLS
BOON

First published in Great Britain 2014
by Mills & Boon, an imprint of Harlequin (UK) Limited,
Eton House, 18-24 Paradise Road, Richmond, Surrey, TW9 1SR

© 2014 Belinda de Rome

ISBN: 978-0-263-24314-7

Harlequin
renewable
sustainabl
to the lega

Printed ar
by CPI Ai

rm

**Avril Tremayne** read *Jane Eyre* as a teenager and has been hooked on tales of passion and romance ever since. An opportunistic insomniac, she has been a lifelong crazy-mad reader, but she took the scenic route to becoming a writer—via gigs as diverse as shoe salesgirl, hot cross bun packer, teacher, and public relations executive. She has spent a good chunk of her life travelling, and has more favourite destinations than should be strictly allowable.

Avril is happily settled in her hometown of Sydney, Australia, where her husband and daughter try to keep her out of trouble—not always successfully. When she's not writing or reading she can generally be found eating—although she does *not* cook!

Check out her website, www.avriltremayne.com, or follow her on Twitter, @AvrilTremayne, and Facebook, www.facebook.com/avril.tremayne

## DEDICATION

This one is for Karen Sloane—
quite possibly the funniest woman on the planet,
and most certainly one of the kindest, most generous
and loyal friends anyone could ask for!

# CHAPTER ONE

*...he tugged at the chignon at her nape. Hairpins scattering, the tight knot unwound. His fingers slid through the heavy chestnut silk—*

'CATHY!'

Catherine North jumped in her seat, scoring a bright red mark across the manuscript page she'd been poring over.

Max.

Her boss.

Back early from his overseas trip.

She cast one horrified glance at her computer screen, where the ardent love moves of her fictional hero, Alex Taylor, screamed *Disaster*! at her. A second glance went to the printer, which was delivering *Passion Flower* page by steamy page at precisely timed intervals.

'Cathy? I'm back!' came the bellow.

Catherine's breath jammed like a fork in her throat. Heart leapt. Sweat popped.

She shoved at the edge of her desk and shot backwards across the floor on her wheeled chair to the printer. Grabbed the pages. Used her feet to leverage another whizzing roll back to her desk. Shuffled the fresh pages behind the others she'd be marking up. Stopped, panting like a woman in labour. What next?

A click from the printer galvanised her. *Duh!* She should have *cancelled the print job* first. She started jabbing, lightning-fast, at the keyboard. *Find the printer.* Jab. *The print queue.* Jab, jab. *Dammit, where is it? Where* is *it? Where—*

She heard a curse, looked up. Saw Max's brown leather briefcase swinging into sight, rounding the corner. Froze as six feet and two inches of lean, elegantly suited frame descended on her with its usual churning impatience.

No time to stop the printer. No time to save her changes. No sudden frantic moves now if she didn't want to look seven shades of guilty.

Catherine dragged in a breath around the fork in her throat as Max came to a stop in front of her desk. A waft of his expensively delicious cologne slid up her nostrils. She looked up at him, smiled serenely, and with an admirable imitation of calm, slid the damning pages under the thick report that was mercifully sitting in her in-tray.

'Good morning, Mr Rutherford.'

'Huh,' he said. Or maybe asked.

Max had become pretty free lately with that slightly mystified 'huh', but Catherine hadn't worked out what the 'huh' said about his state of mind and she was *not* going to start interpreting it today. She just wanted him to go into his office. Like, right that second.

But he didn't. He just stood there.

Silence. Except for the sound of the printer, relentlessly spitting out pages. Max hadn't looked in that direction yet, but he would.

*Breathe. Think. Breathe.*

She needed a distraction. Something dramatic, to keep his attention from straying over there. Something like… throwing up—if only she didn't have a stomach like cast-iron. Or fainting—which she'd never come close to. Or maybe a heart attack. That was at least a possibility, because her heart was jumping around in her chest so vigorously she thought it might crack a rib.

And then it registered. He hadn't noticed what was happening over at the printer. He hadn't noticed her technically perfect in-tray slide. He hadn't even noticed her 'good morning'.

Because he was too busy noticing her hair.

*Oh, my God.*

Her hair. She raised a hand, touched the loose waves. Felt her eyeballs bug out behind her glasses.

Shock, horror, as it all came rushing back.

Last night. Being so carried away with her writing she hadn't made it to bed until four. Causing her to sleep through her alarm. No time for breakfast. No coffee. Ergo, no wits. Therefore deciding there was no harm in coming to work *au naturel* today.

Just one day—no biggie, because Max was out of town so it didn't matter.

And yet…here he was.

And here *she* was.

At least a disordered version of herself, with swathes of her luxuriant reddish-brown hair, usually ruthlessly disciplined, waving around her face. Wearing a figure-hugging black knit top instead of one of her usual white shirts. Minus the drab cardigan she normally wore—because why swelter in black knit *and* a cardigan in a Sydney summer, when Max was out of town and wouldn't see her?

And then Max's eyes dropped to her chest and Catherine lost it.

'What are you doing here?' she demanded.

'What happened to you?' Max asked simultaneously.

'What do you mean, what happened to me?'

'What do you mean, doing here? I *work* here! I *own* here!'

*Distract, distract, distract.*

Catherine arched an eyebrow. 'Oh, *do* you work here? I'd forgotten, it's been so long.'

They stared at each other.

The click and whirr of the printer continued, depositing pages, layer upon layer.

At last Max flicked a glance at it. 'What the devil are you printing, anyway?'

'A document,' Catherine said, and only just managed not to wince at the inadequacy of that.

'Oh, a *document*. Enlightening.'

'You want me to show you?' *Oh, God. Oh, God. Oh, God.* She was an *idiot*.

He tilted his head, curious. 'Do you *want* to show me?'

Catherine opened her mouth, but no sound came out.

'No? Hmm… Not moonlighting, are you?' Max asked.

*Moonlighting…* Not *exactly*. But she'd be damned if she couldn't build on that as a worthy diversion. She was desperate enough to try it, anyway, in the absence of something more dramatic—meteorite destroying planet Earth, maybe?

She straightened in her seat, nice and huffy. 'You're the moonlighter.'

'What the hell are you talking about?'

She flared an outraged nostril. 'You're doing my job.'

'Huh?'

'Aren't I supposed to make your travel arrangements?'

'Yes, but I don't see—'

'Well, *I* didn't make your travel bookings two weeks ago, and *I* didn't *change* any of your bookings, and yet you were gone, and now you're here, so…?' She raised her hands, palms up, shrugged.

He looked suitably—if uncharacteristically—flustered. 'I just— It just— Look, when I changed my plans there wasn't time to bother you, so I did it myself. It's called being considerate.'

'Mr Rutherford, I like to be kept busy at work.'

'Miss North, I *will keep* you busy.' His eyes strayed towards her chest again, widened fractionally, and then jolted straight back to her face. 'At work,' he tacked on quickly.

Catherine gritted her teeth. 'It's *Ms*!' she said, wishing she could cross her arms over her chest, but scared it would draw his attention back there.

'No, actually, it's Catherine and Max,' he said testily. 'I keep telling you it's not the nineteen-sixties, so knock it off. Seriously, you make me feel a hundred and two instead of thirty-two.'

He didn't wait for a response—luckily, because she didn't have one. Just muttered something unintelligible and grabbed the hefty report from her in-tray.

'I have some notes to give you on this Queensland business, among other things, so come in and we'll see about ensuring you have something to do. If you have the time, that is, *Ms* Catherine.'

And at last he strode into his office.

Danger averted.

Catherine suddenly felt like laughing—partly because the sudden release of tension was such a relief, and partly from the sheer absurdity of that scene. Perhaps the most absurd so far in her four months at Rutherford Property—and there had been *plenty.*

She and Max had the most ridiculous boss-employee relationship. It felt like a theatre production, with each of them playing a role: her the prim, often outraged spinster—which she most definitely was *not*—and Max the irascible autocrat. And she was pretty sure *that* was one big, tough-guy act.

Max thrived on people speaking their minds—mainly because it allowed him to do the same. It made for some hair-raisingly direct and unceremonious exchanges of opinions. It also made work both unpredictable and fun. Catherine figured that was how Max had slipped past her defences; it was just too hard to keep your distance from a boss who actually *wanted* you to be insubordinate.

'Cathy!'

'Yes—coming.' Ruthlessly morphing back into strait-laced assistant mode, Catherine grabbed her compact out of her bag to check her face. She wanted so badly to at least fix her hair. Well, she would just have to be *extra* buttoned-up tomorrow, so Max would think today's unprofessional appearance was a figment of his imagination. And she would *not* make the mistake of coming into the office minus her camouflage gear ever again.

'How long are you going to keep me waiting?'

Max's bark brought her thoughts to an abrupt halt.

'Just one minute,' Catherine said soothingly as she turned off the printer as a shortcut to stopping the job—a feat she accomplished with such suddenness a page jammed.

She cleared the paper tray, swearing under her breath with a fluency that was very unlike Ms North Prudish Secretary—but she was stressed, dammit! She looked like *this*, Max was waiting, she was wasting precious moments unjamming the printer, and she had yet to save the changes she'd made to her manuscript and get it onto the flash drive and off the screen.

At last the sheet pulled free.

*'Catherine!'*

'Two seconds.'

She spun towards the computer, but before she could lower a finger towards the keyboard she heard the unmistakable sound of Max cursing as he pushed back his chair.

He was always so impatient!

Reacting on instinct, she simply hit the off switch, trusting the computer to do a back-up save. Then she pulled out the flash drive and thrust it to the back of her top drawer, snatched up her notepad, grabbed a pencil and hurried towards Max's office—managing to run straight into him.

Catherine was too shocked at the sudden contact even to recoil as Max's hands shot out to steady her.

It was the first time Max had touched her—and the fact that it was purely accidental did nothing to stop the heat that sizzled through her body in a fierce surge.

For one moment Max froze. Then his hands dropped. 'Are you okay?'

'I told you I was on my way in,' she said, staring at his chest so he wouldn't see how rattled she was. 'You didn't have to come barrelling out like a rodeo rider on a bull.'

'You were taking too long.'

'You're too impatient,' she said.

Pause. And then, 'What's so interesting about my shirt?'

Catherine sucked in a breath, thinking fast. 'Actually, it's your tie,' she said.

'Is there something *wrong* with my tie?'

She managed a sorry-but-you-did-ask look up. 'Yes. It's *mauve*. Isn't mauve a bit poncy?'

He hooted out a laugh, and Catherine's breath became all jammed up because she wanted to laugh, too, whenever *he* did.

'Ouch! Weight-lifting tonight, then, to get my macho back.'

Another laugh. Delighted.

Catherine's fingers went for the top button of her shirt— her first line of defence in reminding herself of exactly who she was in this office. But, encountering skin above fine wool instead, her fingers hovered there ineffectually.

'No button today,' Max observed. His eyes followed her hand as it fluttered up to her earlobe, searching for her second line of defence. 'And no little gold hoops. What are you going to do now?'

Well, what she was *not* going to do was get into a discussion about the way she looked! 'Work, I assume, Mr Rutherford,' she said.

'Max,' he said.

Catherine blinked at him. 'I know what your first name is.'

'Then *use* it, dammit.'

Catherine's resistance to calling her boss by his first name had become quite a bone of contention. It just felt too...too *personal*. And she didn't like personal in the office. Personal could move into unsafe territory if you weren't on your guard. And she was already teetering on the edge with *Passion Flower*.

But she decided not to antagonise him with another 'Mr Rutherford' for the rest of the day.

'All right,' she said. 'Max.'

He looked shocked for a moment—but then he nodded, satisfied. *Too* satisfied.

'But please don't swear at me,' she added, very saintly, and almost gave herself away by giggling as his satisfaction gave way to bemusement.

'But I didn't sw—' He broke off, and slowly his bone-melting lopsided smile appeared. 'Oh, the "dammit".' He laughed. 'Sometimes I wonder if you're really as twinset-and-pearls as you'd have me believe, Cathy.'

'Twinset and pearls?'

'Prim and proper.'

A strangled sound escaped Catherine, and Max looked at her sharply.

She quickly schooled her features into an appropriately offended expression. 'I do own a twinset and pearls, actually,' she said, with the hint of a sniff. Of course nobody who'd seen her fire-engine-red cashmere twinset had ever described it as anything other than 'hot'. And the pearls were exotic *black* pearls, interspersed with eye-popping turquoise.

They'd been given to her on her twenty-first birthday, five years before, by her hang-gliding, motorbike-riding brother, Luke, and had cost half the impressive advance he'd received for his second crime novel. To describe those pearls as anything other than dazzling would be ludicrous.

Max dipped his head in that way he had when he wanted to look her in the eye. And look he did—as though trying to dive into her brain through her pupils.

'I wonder why that's so amusing to you?' he asked softly. 'And what you're not telling me?'

Any desire Catherine had to giggle was gone. Sucked out of her by the arrested tone of Max's voice. His utter stillness. That look… So intense…

As though he knew…

No, he *couldn't* know.

Not about her. And not about the book. She'd been so careful to look like, act like, *be* the quintessential strait-laced wallflower. She'd even changed her perfume from dark musk to lemon-scented, to reinforce the impression that she was tart and astringent and not to be touched. And the book was nowhere to be seen. Safely secret.

So if Max thought he was going to dig below her carefully constructed surface with a keen look and a so-soft question he had another think coming.

'Shall we get started?' she asked briskly.

But Max's eyes had dropped, all the way to her feet, and Catherine almost groaned. She'd stuck her nail through her last pair of black tights putting them on in a rush this morning, and—of course—hadn't wanted to take the time to stop and buy more on her way to work. So her legs were bare, and she'd gone all 'what the hell?' and was wearing open-toed shoes, with her red toenails on display.

'Huh,' he said, as if he was saying it to himself.

Catherine fought off a blush. 'Well? Shall we? Get started?'

Max shoved a hand through his already dishevelled hair. His hair was regularly subjected to an unceremonious scrabbling of his hands through it. When he was thinking hard. Or coming up with a brilliant idea. Or exasperated. Or bored. Or... Well, anything.

'Yes, if you can hurry the hell up,' he said, and went striding back into his office.

For the next hour Max talked. About the company's diamond-themed African development, new hotel and shopping complex in Canada and eco-resort in Brazil. Catherine knew how Max worked—his rhythms, his style, his expectations—and could second-guess him as she made notes about actions he wanted put in place, meetings to be arranged, documents to chase up. She took a little old-fashioned dictation for some correspondence, but Max always expected her to finesse his letters using her own words, so she didn't get too strict with the transcribing, even though she was pretending to get every single syllable verbatim—because that way she could keep her eyes very deliberately *on* her notepad, and *off* her boss.

Which was not easy. Because Max was drop-dead gorgeous.

Just under the too-tall threshold, with the promise of athlete-grade strength under his immaculate suits; black hair on the long side, and always, *always* bed-head tousled; vivid blue eyes fringed with thick, black lashes; that lopsided grin that would turn a female ice sculpture into a puddle.

The whole package—the looks, the sense of humour, the ace brain, and that elusive factor X that made him seem unattainable without any apparent aloofness—was droolworthy.

There was a good side and a bad side to having a hot-as-Hades boss.

The good side? Max had women throwing themselves at him with a frequency and ardour that was embarrassing. He didn't have to grope or flash or proposition an unwilling employee to get his sexual thrills. And what a blissful realisation *that* had been after the hell of her last boss—the despicable RJ Harrow.

But the bad side—and it was very, *very* bad!—was that a month into the job Catherine had started wondering what Max would do if she groped or flashed or propositioned *him*! And she just could not get her head around how she could think like that. The *last* thing Catherine needed was another boss-related fracas, ending in her ignominious departure from a job she was good at.

Not that Max would ever give her the *chance* to grope or flash or proposition him. Because he might be the flirt of the century—as the whole office knew!—but Catherine North wasn't his type. Tall, leggy, blonde—dared she say horsey?—*that* was his type.

She swallowed a giggle as she pictured the shock on Max's face if starchy-knickered Ms North were to roll a prurient eye in his direction. They'd need a defibrillator! Or maybe she could give him mouth-to-mouth...

'Something funny, Cathy? Because you're allowed to laugh here, you know.'

She looked up. 'Nothing's funny.'

He did that through-the-pupils stare, then leaned back in his chair and loosened his tie with three sharp tugs. 'Onto the problem child—Kurrangii, our luxury resort in Queensland.'

He nudged the report he'd taken from her in-tray earlier and smiled at her—and Catherine's heart started knocking into her ribs again as she hastily dropped her eyes and started taking notes.

'*Our*' luxury resort. And it *did* feel as if it was theirs—his and hers—because they'd worked so closely on it together.

That night two weeks ago, when they'd stayed late to finish preparing the main report, Max had loosened his tie with those exact three tugs. Her memory of that night was so clear. Just the two of them, bouncing ideas back and forth, writing and rewriting. They'd ordered in Thai food and worked while they ate. It had struck midnight, but they'd worked on. Neither of them had been happy with the end result, so they'd decided to call it a night and do it all over again the next day—into the night if required.

But Max hadn't turned up the next day. Or the next, or the next, or... Well, he hadn't shown up until today. And in the interim the only contact they'd had was via email or through his deputy, Damian.

It had driven Catherine a little bit crazy.

She'd figured she had two options for dealing with the situation: she could gnash her teeth at her own stupidity for mooning over her *boss*, of all people—and, moreover, one who liked tall, skinny, amenable blondes, not short, curvy, argumentative brunettes—or she could take affirmative action to get her out-of-control hormones back in their cage before he returned.

In the end she'd gone hybrid and started writing *Passion Flower*. A teeth-gnashing way of exploring her secret fascination with Max and hopefully getting it out of her system before she did something really insane—like throwing herself at him and begging him to take her on his desk.

*Ooohh*, a desk scene! Could she write that...?

Catherine realised Max had finished dictating and was

sitting there, watching her, and closed her notepad with a snap.

'So, Cathy...' he said.

His voice sounded raw, and Catherine's mind switched instantly to the job. 'You need water,' she said, standing. 'I'll get it.'

'Huh?'

'Water.'

'Huh?' he said again, and then gave his head a tiny shake.

'Your voice sounds hoarse.'

'No, it's fine,' he said irritably. 'And I can get my own damned water—you're not a servant.' He cleared his throat. 'So, anyway... The Queensland resort. I want to know what you think of all that.'

'All that?' Catherine repeated, sitting again.

'Yes, all that. I wasn't talking to myself, was I? Or maybe I was—because you don't normally sit there like a spewed-up piece of basalt rock.'

'Spewed-up basalt?' she spluttered, caught between laughter and outrage.

'Yeah—like out of a volcano. But where's the molten stuff? Aren't you going to rip into me about the...the...' He stopped, searching for words, shrugged. 'I don't know—the native animals or something?'

'I don't *rip into* you!' she said. 'About anything.'

He laughed. 'Now, *that's* a lie.'

Catherine eyed him cautiously as he stood and walked around the desk, each step redolent with the prowling energy that distinguished all his movements. He stopped just to the side of her chair, then perched his gorgeous butt on the edge of his desk.

'Well? Native animals?' He plucked the notepad out of her hand, flicked through it.

Catherine shifted her chair backwards fractionally, clamping down on a spurt of temper. She'd had plenty to say on that subject already, as Max very well knew, because he forgot *nothing*, so what was this? Torture Your Personal Assistant Day?

She looked at one of Max's slashing black eyebrows, which seemed safer than an actual eyeball. 'Sorry—am I supposed to be allowing for your jet lag? Because you know what I think about that. You thought the same—and you've already addressed the issue.'

'Oh, yeah, we talked about it at length didn't we?' Pause. 'That night before I left for Canada. Right?'

That night. Catherine repeated those words in her head. *That* night—when she'd half wondered, half feared, that short, curvy, argumentative brunettes might actually get a look-in after all—and had ended up sexually frustrated, writing *Passion Flower*.

'Okay, then,' he went on, when Catherine remained silent. 'What's your opinion of the *way* I've addressed it? Will the changes I've recommended damage your perception of the resort? Does it seem less upmarket if the cabins are repositioned the way I just described and the layout and style are modified? Would you still go there?'

'Yes, I'd still go. If I could afford to, I mean—which I can't. So, no, I won't go there, but I would.'

Catherine mentally slapped herself. Could that be the stupidest thing she'd ever said in her life?

'Because...? You would still go because...?' he prompted. 'I'm not asking you for the answer to global warming, Cathy—just a simple opinion about the modifications.'

Her eyes flashed. 'I would still go *because*, judging by the diagrams Carl was kind enough to show me while you were away, the redesign will actually be more in tune with the surroundings. More special. More...secret... That's the way I'd describe it. Which feels more exclusive.'

Max held her notepad out to her. 'Perfect. Put something like that in that last letter, will you? One more meeting on the environmental impact study—just a formality—and we should be ready to get things underway.'

She reached for the notepad and her knee accidentally

brushed against the side of Max's leg. Somehow that made her start to tremble. Sexual frustration alive and kicking!

Next thing Max was tossing her notepad behind him onto the desk and catching her hand in his. Four whole months without physical contact, and in one morning three separate hits?

Today just *sucked.*

'You're shaking,' he said, his face full of concern. 'And you've hardly said a word for the past hour. Something's wrong. Are you ill?'

'No, I'm not ill,' she snapped. 'Nothing's wrong.'

Max looked disbelieving.

'I'm fine,' she insisted, but he clearly wasn't convinced.

Catherine tried to pull her hand free. 'A bit tired, that's all,' she offered.

'Tired? Why?'

*Oh, for God's sake.*

'Just a…a late night.'

She wondered what Max would say if she gave him the bald truth: *A late night transferring a few sexual fantasies about you from my head to the page.* Yeah—maybe not.

He let go of her hand—*whew*!—and folded his arms so his hands were jammed under his armpits.

'Oh. A late night. I thought maybe—' He shook his head. 'Nothing. Must be lunchtime, right? I assume you have…' Another clearing of the throat. 'Do you have plans?'

She got to her feet with alacrity. 'Yes, I do.'

He watched her for a long moment. X-ray eyes.

Catherine's hand reached for the button that wasn't there, and at last Max waved her towards the door. 'Can you be back by one-thirty?'

'Yes, of course,' Catherine said, and dodged around him to grab her notepad.

She hurried from the office as Max reefed the report he'd taken from her in-tray off the desk, as though it would bite him if he didn't subdue it.

Typical Max! He never just picked something up—he had to throttle it.

Back at her desk, Catherine neatened her work area mechanically. Simmering at the back of her mind was the worrying certainty that her working relationship with Max had gone off the rails this morning. That she'd been caught out.

*Something's wrong. Are you ill?*

*Yes, I'm sick with lust! What are you going to do about it?*

He'd bypass the thermometer and go straight for the psychiatrist if he knew the truth.

She heard a curse float out from his office. He always cursed and tore his hands through his hair when something outside his control slowed him down, so he must have seen something wrong in the report.

She caught herself smiling, and pinched her lips to stop it. What the hell was there to smile at? If there was something wrong in the report Max had only himself to blame, because he'd choofed off to Canada instead of sticking around to beat it into shape.

And him choofing off to Canada was none of her business. She wished he'd go *back* to Canada. She wished he'd *relocate* to Canada and *email* his work in. Because it was *not* 'our' resort. It was *his* resort. And she would do well to remember that. Sharp, clear distinction between work and personal. Because work wasn't personal. Work was *work*.

And, now she thought of it, she was going to change that scene in *Passion Flower*. That scene with Alex and Jennifer working in the office over a Thai meal—which she would make a...a...a *Chinese* meal. In fact she would delete the whole scene. Because in reality that interlude had ended with a brusque 'Thank you for your help' and a drive away—and what was so romantic about *that*? What did she think she was doing, turning *that* into a *'Jenny, do you know how long I've wanted you?'* moment, complete with a slow reel in and a soft kiss?

She was a freaking *idiot*!

And her damned book *sucked*.

'Sucked': word of the day.

Her eyes moved to her in-tray, where her dark secret was buried.

*Uh-oh.* Where her dark secret was *not* buried.

Because the manuscript was sitting brazenly on top.

A whoosh of panic had her reaching for the back of her chair to steady herself. Until she remembered that the report had been covering it and Max had taken the report. That was the only reason the book was sitting there exposed.

Nothing to panic over.

Until she reached out to grab the pages so she could stick them in her briefcase…and saw the page on top.

She distinctly remembered scoring a red mark on the page when Max had called her name.

But there was no red mark on the page.

Catherine's heart stopped, then started pounding. She slid into her chair, boneless. Flicked through her in-tray again. Sat stock-still for one appalled moment.

No red mark anywhere.

So…if the report had been on top of the manuscript, that meant…

*No—God, no.* Max Rutherford had picked up a few pages of her book along with his report!

And Max had started reading that report as she was leaving the office.

Hot, then cold, then hot. Hyperventilation. Paper bag… she needed a paper bag. Brain not working. Brain dead.

Then adrenaline tore through her veins and her synapses fired—electrified by pure fear—and she latched on to two essential facts: *one*, if Max had read even one sentence of those pages he would have come screeching out already and, *two*, she had to get those pages back.

Get them back *immediately*. But without running into his office, waving her arms and looking like an insane asylum escapee.

*Breathe. Breathe. Breathe.*

Nope—there was nothing for it. It was physically impossible for her to walk calmly into Max's office.

She was going in like an insane person.

# CHAPTER TWO

MAX SIGHED, UNWILLING to give up until he'd read every page of the report—even if he had yet to take in a single word.

His mind wasn't on it. His mind wasn't in the office at all. His mind was at lunch.

But he wasn't going to acknowledge *whose* lunch his mind was at, or *why* it was there. Because he was a moron, and had done nothing right for two weeks, and nothing had *felt* right the whole time he'd been away, and enough was enough, and it was time to put his mind back where it should be.

So he just sat at his desk, flipping, skimming, flipping, skimming. Counting down pages until he found a word he could take in: 'Conclusion'.

One rush of air later he found himself holding nothing.

The report had been whisked out of his hands so fast it took a few seconds for him to feel the sting of the paper cut that had just been inflicted in the web between his thumb and his index finger.

'Ouch!'

He looked up.

Catherine. Looking horrified.

That was…weird.

Catherine North never looked anything but completely composed. At least she hadn't until today.

But, then again, Catherine North had never worn figure-hugging black that emphasised every mind-numbingly deli-cious curve until today. And Catherine North had never let a glossy, finger-luring curl stray out of place until today. And Catherine North had never had the skin of her legs visible until today. And Catherine North—

Was *definitely* looking horrified.

'Lunch date stand you up?' he couldn't resist asking, wondering if there was a more direct way he could ask her who she was having lunch with without making himself look more of a moron than he already was.

Eyes huge behind the lenses of her tortoiseshell-rimmed spectacles, Catherine shook her head.

She didn't seem inclined to add anything, so Max asked, 'Did you want that report for a particular reason?'

He watched, fascinated, as the tip of her tongue came out to scoot quickly across her bottom lip.

She had the sexiest bottom lip he'd ever seen.

'No,' she said, and the bottom lip pinched itself in, in its usual repressed fashion.

Still looked sexy, though.

Max sucked a drop of blood from his wound, waiting to hear what Catherine would add. But it seemed no more information was forthcoming. 'Then do you think I could have it back?' he asked politely.

'It?'

'The report.'

'Of course,' she said, looking down as she hived off some pages from the back and held the rest out to him. She turned quickly on her heel.

Before she could take a step, Max asked, 'Don't I get to look at those pages, too?'

She stopped. Her shoulders tightened. And then she shrugged and said over her shoulder, 'Just some shredding you picked up by mistake with the report. I wanted to take care of it before I left for lunch.'

And then she was running out.

And Catherine North had never run *anywhere* in this office. Until today.

So... What was so special about today?

Max's mouth turned down. In short—nothing.

His return to the office had been monumentally disappointing. Not that he'd had any business expecting anything to be different just because he'd been away for two weeks and they'd left things a little...

*Ugh.* A little *nothing*! That was how they'd left things.

They'd worked hard that night, and she'd been so gobsmackingly smart, and warm, and energised, and it had been *great*. Like a revelation. No, not a revelation—a *confirmation*...of something he'd always suspected. That Catherine was...special.

And then they'd taken the elevator down to the car park and he'd said, 'Thank you for your help,' and she'd said, 'No problem,' and they'd looked at each other... One, two, three, four beats.

And then they'd gone to their cars and driven off.

And he'd flown to Canada as fast as he'd been able to book and go.

Yep, he really was a moron.

'Moron': word of the day. And it was all his.

He went back to page one of the report.

Two minutes later he was cursing and slamming it down again. He was getting nowhere. And all because Catherine was...different. As if something had changed.

Running away to Canada without telling her had obviously been a mistake. But he'd just been...cautious. No, he was never cautious. More like *reluctant*. Reluctant to mess around with their excellent working relationship by giving in to his curiosity about her. Curiosity about what it would be like to—

*No!* He shot to his feet. He would *not* go there, even in his head.

He started pacing around the office, letting out some excess energy.

*Not going there.* Because it was one thing flirting in the office when you both knew the score, but quite another to hit on a strait-laced virgin who was *not interested*. Even his father, serial secretary-dater and all-round loser, didn't go there.

And Ms North was not *remotely* interested. Ms North did not know the meaning of the word 'flirt'. Ms North would skewer him with a letter-opener if he laid a lukewarm look on her, let alone a questing finger. Look at the way she'd freaked when he'd held her fingers for a couple of seconds— as if he was an eagle and she was a tiny bird struggling to get free of his talons. And the reception he'd got on arrival today, which had given new meaning to the word 'unwelcome'. She'd even had it in for his new tie.

He looked down at his tie, decided she was right, and tugged it off. Laughed again as he went back to his desk and sat down.

And then he wondered if he was going mad, laughing about his tie in the middle of this mess. His hands went diving into his hair. It— No, she! *She* was so...so *frustrating*.

At first it had been a novelty, having an assistant who wasn't remotely interested in his body.

But it had moved past that, to another novelty: being seriously attracted to someone who looked as if she'd faint if she heard the word 'sex'.

Even without today's hair and top and toenails—even when she was buttoned to the hilt in ill-fitting shirts covered with drab cardigans in shades of porridge and grey and dinge-green—he'd started feeling a little tortured—but in a weirdly good way—being near her.

That lemony fresh perfume she wore combined with her natural scent beneath it—lovely. The way her luminous hazel eyes shone behind her lenses when she was arguing her case—adorable. The habit she had of touching the button at her collar as though reassuring herself it was done up— intriguing. And when her fingers sneaked up to her perfectly shaped ear to touch the discreet gold hoop—demure...and yet somehow *not* demure.

He cursed under his breath, reached for the report again and saw another tiny bead of blood from the paper cut. He grabbed a tissue from the box on his desk and blotted it. Frowned at his hand as he remembered the look on Catherine's face. There had been something at the bottom of the report Catherine hadn't wanted him to see.

Max thought back again to his arrival that morning. He'd been so shocked at how she looked he'd been blinded to anything else at first. But if he dug past that there had been... dismay. No, *more* than dismay. She hadn't wanted him anywhere near her. Because of...

The printing!

She'd been on edge because—and the truth was slapping him in the face now—he'd disturbed her printing something she shouldn't have been printing. She hadn't wanted to tell him what the document was—not that he'd really cared; he'd only asked because she'd looked so guilty. He'd wanted to goad her a little, get one of those mind-your-own-business glares out of her that just cracked him up. But now...?

What would a personal assistant be printing that her boss shouldn't see? What would have her running in and snatching it out of his hands? Hmm...

Oh. *Oh!* Well, of course. A job application!

But she'd been printing reams. Too long for a letter and CV.

So not just one job. More than one. Which meant she wasn't attracted to a special job she'd just happened upon but wanting to leave *this* job and going all-out scattergun to do it. God knew how many emails she'd sent to complement so many snail-mail CVs.

It was like an arrow between the eyes, and for a full minute he couldn't think straight.

And then he *could* think. But his poor benumbed brain seemed willing to accommodate only one thought: Catherine wasn't allowed to leave.

He forced himself to put that ironclad fact to one side. Because if his bogged brain didn't start working how was he going to figure out a way to make her stay?

*Just ask her to!*

Okay, that seemed logical—although how he could do it out of the blue, when she hadn't actually indicated she was unhappy with her job, was not immediately obvious.

Except... *Damn.* She'd said today she couldn't afford to go to Kurrangii. Had to be a message in that. *He wasn't paying her enough.*

Well, he could give her a pay rise. It was his company— he could pay her whatever he wanted. Whatever *she* wanted!

Good. Perfect solution.

Without further ado he was out of his chair and heading for the door. 'Catherine!' he bellowed, before he reached it.

Silence.

He bolted through the doorway, searching.

Empty.

Max leaned against the doorjamb, running both hands into his hair. Why hadn't he asked her where she was going for lunch? *Hello? Earth to Max? Irrelevant!* As if he could invade her date to offer her a pay rise! He'd look completely deranged.

Dammit. He was going to have to wait until she got back. He *hated* waiting.

He checked his watch. Forty minutes.

Feeling he should be doing *something*, he circled her desk. Looking at its almost stately tidiness made him smile. It was strangely comforting to see the evidence of her fastidious little habits.

His brain went stubborn on him for the second time: Catherine wasn't allowed to leave.

Of course if he had a copy of what she'd been printing he'd be in a better position to know what he was up against. What counter-offer would work.

But there was no paper on the desk. No paper anywhere. Reflexively, his gaze moved to the printer. Clean. Silent. Turned off. The computer, too. Strange.

He sat in her chair. Looked at the computer screen. Turned on the computer and signed in to the system.

A sudden mental picture of how he looked—at Cathe-

rine's desk, in her chair, hunched in front of her computer—
made him roll his eyes. Thank God their suite of offices was
completely private, so nobody would wander past and see
him in this shameful Machiavellian guise. But, even so, this
was crazy! What had he come to? He should just wait for
her to come back and *ask* her what was going on! The way
a *sane* person would.

He reached to flick the computer off.

And saw it.

A document. Recovered—the way it happened when you
turned off the computer suddenly. Just there on the screen,
without him searching or opening anything. A document
called... What the *hell*...?

'Passion Flower'.

*Passion Flower?*

Max looked around, feeling a tad uncomfortable now
the moment of truth had arrived and it turned out not to be
a job application—because nobody called a job application
*Passion Flower.*

Could he really do this?

It took him perhaps two seconds to decide that, yes, he
could. He had a right to read any document he wanted—this
was his business, these were his premises, it was his equipment. Really, he was honour-bound to look.

Three seconds after that he started reading. But he wasn't
prepared for the reality.

Underneath the title *Passion Flower* was a line in smaller
type. It read: *A novel of love, lust and loneliness.*

And Max's jaw dropped.

*Jennifer Andrews had been dreaming of her boss for
months. Wild, erotic dreams.*

Definitely not a job application, Max thought, shell-
shocked. No way was he going to stop, though.

He read, scrolled, read, scrolled.

He'd figured out the truth as soon as he'd clapped eyes

on that strapline, but somehow it wasn't until he arrived at page three that the knowledge crystallised into recognisable syllables.

Cathy was writing a novel.

A romance novel.

A *sexy* romance novel.

He scrolled again, avidly searching, the sentences and phrases beckoning to him like a siren's call, wrapping around his senses.

> *She knew Alex would be back soon, but Jennifer was too impatient to sit calmly in the navy leather chair she always occupied.*

Navy leather chair! Like the chairs in *his* office, where Cathy sat.

> *She was drawn to Alex's office window. Ten floors down, Jennifer could see the Botanic Gardens. It felt like a scene trapped in time...the immaculate green of the trees...Sydney Harbour shining in the distance, a diamond-sprinkled sheet of blue silk...the sun radiating a heady, hazy aphrodisiac...*

Tenth floor. Office window overlooking the Botanic Gardens. Sydney Harbour. Check, check, check.

> *Alex walked into the office, brown briefcase in hand, and fixed her with his blue-eyed stare.*
> *'Notepad, Jenny,' he barked at her.*

Max was incapable of stopping his fingers from hitting the down arrow as his eyes stayed glued to the monitor to see what would happen next.

> *Alex towered over her, six feet two inches from the top of his tousled black hair to his Italian leather shoes.*

*She clutched the red silk of her peignoir against her chest...*

Max's finger kept punching the down arrow, almost obsessively.

A red silk peignoir...

What would Cathy look like in *that*?

Max breathed out and sat back in Catherine's chair to recover the breath that had somehow become linked to an almost savage tightening in his groin.

He checked his watch, assessing how much time he had. A twinge of conscience hit him. He should not be reading this. He should stop. This was bad.

But he returned his finger, now a little shaky, to the keyboard.

Catherine was determined to be back at precisely one-thirty, as ordered, so she hurried her friend and colleague Nell through lunch fast enough to cause dyspepsia.

'What's the rush?' Nell protested as Catherine all but grabbed a passing waiter by the apron to demand the bill before they'd finished their coffee. 'Max isn't going to mind if you're late.'

'*I'll* mind. And would you stop staring at me? I've had enough of that from Max!'

'Well, it's such a change.' Nell gulped a mouthful of coffee. 'What did he say? Max? About the new you?'

'Nothing of consequence.'

Which was the truth. Not that it was really the 'new' her; it was the *old* her—not that anybody at Rutherford Property could possibly know that.

'And, anyway, remember the girlfriends? Susie, Maria, Leah? All tall, all blonde, all dressed in tight, short dresses? And that was just in my first month. And the parade of starry-eyed PAs before me? All tall, blonde, blah-blah-blah?'

'Haven't seen any of his famous blondes for a while.'

'Oh, he'll have one stashed somewhere. And, regardless,

he wouldn't notice me—not in the way you mean—if I burst into his office doing the Dance of the Seven Veils.'

Catherine delved into her purse and laid some notes on the table without waiting for the bill. 'I'm paying—the least I can do after rushing you into a bout of indigestion. But can we go? Like…now? Right now?'

'All right,' Nell said, 'but I still don't get why we have to hurry. We're not late.'

Catherine didn't plan on enlightening her—because she couldn't explain, even to herself, the unformed sense of panic that had been racing through her veins ever since she'd left the office. Telling herself that everything was fine and she was merely suffering from a guilty conscience and an over-active imagination didn't seem to be working. And the panic just kept growing.

Catherine bade Nell a preoccupied farewell at level eight and, the moment she was alone in the elevator, jabbed irritably at the button for level ten. Although she knew the elevator wouldn't ascend any faster just because she hit the button a thousand times.

She breathed a sigh of relief when the doors opened at her floor—only to choke on it as she rounded the corner from the lift lobby.

Max was sitting in her chair, eyes glued to her computer screen.

*Ohhhhhhhh.*

Not much of a thought, but all she could manage initially.

She reminded herself that she'd turned everything off, that the flash drive was in her drawer, the printed pages shoved in her briefcase, and there was no way he could be looking at *Passion Flower*. He was probably looking for the Queensland report to make some changes.

*So breathe. Breathe and be normal.*

'Is there something you wanted urgently?' she asked, forcing herself not to run to her desk but to walk slowly, calmly.

Max raised his head and looked at her—slack-jawed, marvelling, astounded.

And Catherine knew.

Max's voice, when it finally came, was unbelievably husky. 'You wrote this?'

# CHAPTER THREE

CATHERINE'S BRAIN WAS limping around the edges of semi-formed words, refusing to fasten on to any of them long enough for her to string a response together.

Max shook his head, as if he'd sustained a blow and was reeling. 'You wrote this.' This time it wasn't a question.

Automatically Catherine's hand moved to where her top button should have been primly done up.

Max's stunned eyes followed her hand—could he see her pulse throbbing there?—moved lower, lower. Until every inch of her had been examined.

Catherine was lost—no button, no earrings. Coping the next best way, she whipped off her glasses and started polishing them ineffectually.

*Thinking. Thinking. Thinking.*

*"'His fingers slid through the heavy chestnut silk as he looked down at her, his vivid blue gaze on Jennifer's hazel eyes through the round tortoiseshell rims of her spectacles...'"* Max recited, watching her as though spellbound.

He knew it by heart! Catherine put her glasses back on and took the only route open to her: she threw herself on her sword with an unvarnished 'I'm sorry.'

'Sorry?'

'For bringing it here—doing it at work. I've just...just had a lot of time on my hands lately, while you've been travelling.' Catherine braced herself for the inevitable: she was going to get the sack. She deserved it. She stiffened her spine and said again, 'I'm sorry.'

But apparently Max was too stunned to respond. All he could do was stare.

And it was unbearable. Yes, she was three hundred per cent in the wrong—crush on her boss—*groan*—turning him into Alex—*ugh*—bringing the book to work and using Max's equipment, supplies and the time he was paying for—*cringe*. But come *on*! Do the humane thing and drop the axe, get it over with—sack her, tell her to—

'Why?' Max asked suddenly.

Oh. A word at last. But not what she was expecting.

'Because,' Catherine said.

Clearly she wasn't going to win any prizes for writing snappy dialogue with a comeback like that—but what the hell *was* that? *Why?* Why *what*? Why was she sorry? Why was she writing it? Why was it in the office?

She had a vision of that meteorite she'd wished for earlier, plummeting towards the earth, targeting the Sydney Central Business District.

Max stood slowly, like a man in a dream. His eyes did another slow rove along her body before he walked around her desk and stopped beside her.

'And you...' he breathed, still visibly stunned. 'She's you. Jennifer Andrews is you. The chestnut hair, the glasses, the hazel eyes—you're Jennifer.'

Catherine wasn't going to bother denying it. But she wasn't going to confirm it either. And, in any case, she was too busy trying to form a reply to what she just *knew* his next question—the *important* question—would be.

'So who's the tall, black-haired, blue-eyed man? Who's Alex?'

Yep. Next question—right on cue. Because Max wasn't an idiot.

'I made him up,' Catherine said, too quickly, backing away a step.

'You didn't draw on a flesh-and-blood model?'

Catherine fingered one naked earlobe. 'N-not too…too heavily. Not really.'

'You seem a little flustered, Cathy,' Max said, softly, closing the distance again.

Catherine wondered if the air between them, impregnated with his scent, had some mysterious connection to her insides. Because she sure felt strange, breathing it in.

'I just don't want you to think I'm—'

Catherine heard the pathetic squeak that had replaced her voice and stopped herself. *Enough.* Catherine North did not do pathetic squeaks—not old Catherine, not new Catherine, not *any* Catherine.

She took a deep breath, settled herself. 'I know I shouldn't be working on personal matters in the office,' she said, and was pleased with that businesslike steering of the conversation into more appropriate waters. Because, really, it was her less than professional behaviour that should be the topic under discussion here—not the colour of her eyes or the model for her hero! 'So I'm sorry.'

*For the third time, and now can you just sack me?*

'You described the gardens perfectly,' Max said, uncooperatively. 'I've often wondered what you look at when you gaze out of my office window. You do it a lot, you know.'

'I do? Ah… Well, I…I do draw on real life for descriptions of…of places. Now, could we—'

'And my leather chairs?'

'The setting is…is incidental. It has no bearing on anything. I just…just like those chairs. And they seemed…' Catherine's words dried up as Max continued to look at her with that slightly dazed and wholly speculative expression.

'So. Black hair, blue eyes, six-two.' He repeated the description slowly. 'What does he do for a living, I wonder? Engineer, by any chance?'

The flare of horror in Catherine's eyes must have confirmed that nicely for him, because he grinned.

'Lots of men are engineers,' she said.

*Uh-oh*, little squeak there.

'Shall we start eliminating the ones with brown or green eyes? The fair-haired engineers? The short ones? And the engineers who—?'

'Look, Alex Taylor is a figment of my imagination,' Catherine said shortly, and walked stiffly past Max to put her bag in the cupboard. She sat in her chair, whipped her hair back, coiled it into as tight a knot as she could and stuck a pencil through it to hold it. Better. 'Now, are you going to sack me or not?'

'Huh?' He stared at her. 'Don't be stupid. Of course I'm not going to sack you.'

She closed her eyes, just briefly, to savour the relief of that. 'Then shall we get back to work? You *did* say I was going to be busy.'

Max leaned over her desk, arms straight, hands flat on the wood either side of hers, where they were clutching the nearest thing she could find—which happened to be a stapler.

'He's me, isn't he?' Max asked.

Catherine laughed, as though that were too silly to consider.

But Max apparently wasn't going to be sidetracked, and she didn't blame him after that unconvincing titter.

'Well?' he prompted.

'The book is fiction,' she said. Well, that was actually the truth! 'The characters are made up.' Okay—that part was a lie. 'Now, can we get back to reality?' And *that* was the important thing.

Max leaned closer. Catherine could smell his spicy cologne. Vanilla, a touch of sandalwood, a hint of amber. Heaven.

'Sure we can,' he said. 'Fiction is fun, Catherine, but the real world is where it's at.'

Catherine accidentally stapled her thumb, but didn't feel it.

The real world... The world RJ Harrow had opened her eyes to. Where bosses tried to get their assistants into bed and if the assistant said no her life became a living hell.

Where she got waylaid in corridors and shoved against walls and mauled in hotel rooms and there was nothing she could do about it because apparently it was her own fault for looking the way she did.

The real world *sucked*—hello, word of the day! That was the whole point of *Passion Flower.* So there was no confusing reality with fantasy. Because in *Passion Flower* the assistant could say whatever she damned well wanted: yes, no, maybe, drop dead.

But of course in *Passion Flower,* bespectacled, hazeleyed personal assistant Jennifer said a passionate *yes* to tall, black-haired, blue-eyed Alex the engineer.

And now Max had read all about that passionate *yes.* Max knew she was Jennifer. Knew he was Alex. Did that mean…? Did Max think Catherine was asking for it? Because of what happened in the book? Because of the way she looked today? Because of that night, two weeks ago, when she'd let her guard down?

Max was doing that through-the-pupils-into-the-brain stare while he waited for her to say something, but she was incapable of speech.

And then he leaned a smidgeon closer. 'Cathy, there's one thing. About Alex. He's not quite—'

'You've completely misunderstood,' she said, cutting him off.

She calmly removed the staple from her thumb, as though she regularly stapled a body part, and repositioned the stapler back on the desk.

'Alex Taylor is a…a composite. The black hair comes from a man whose name is Luke. And then there's my neighbour, Rick, who has the most amazing amber eyes—because, you see, I am in the process of changing Alex's eyes from blue to amber; it's a much more unusual colour, you know. And the engineer part is from all the Rutherford Property guys—you, of course, and Damian, *and* Carl.'

'*Carl?*'

'Yes, Carl—who is brilliant if only you'd look past his

shyness. Really brilliant—and kind, and creative. Did you know he paints?'

'No, I didn't,' Max snapped. And—thank *God*—he removed his hands from her desk and straightened. He plucked a ruler off her desk and started flexing it.

There was silence as Max stared at her, flexing the ruler. Flexing, flexing. And then it snapped, and he looked at it as though he had no idea how it had ended up in his hands.

Her with the stapler, him with the ruler. God help the paperclips, the way they were going!

'Right—composite—got it,' he said. 'But I'm going to have to play the boss card, Catherine, and tell you to direct your attention to something worthwhile while I'm in Queensland for the next week. Like the…the filing. I'd like the old files sorted and archived.'

Catherine's eyes shot to his. She wanted to protest that he'd only just got back after too long away, but she swallowed the words. It wasn't her job to question the boss about his comings and goings—just to book them. And then do the filing while she imagined him with a horse-faced blonde bimbo in his hotel room.

Long, silent growl.

'When would you like your flight booked?' she asked tightly.

'Tomorrow. First flight to Cairns.'

Catherine sat looking at him, wanting to call back the whole disastrous day.

Max's gaze tangled with hers for endless moments.

Suddenly he seemed to come to a conclusion. Forking one hand through his hair, he turned on his heel, broken ruler clenched in one fist, went into his office, and quietly closed the door.

Max had said he'd be gone a week. But he was now two days overdue. And it was driving Catherine nuts.

Once Max had left for Queensland he'd reverted to passing on his instructions via Damian, responding to her phone messages via text or email and not once actually speaking to her.

Catherine tossed another pile of old files onto her desk for sorting. She *hated* filing! She hated *everything*. Her head was aching because she'd been pinning her hair too tightly for a week and two days. She was wearing thicker tights and they were making her itch. She'd bought new shirts that buttoned so high they were choking her. All to counteract the *Passion Flower* effect.

The least Max could do was show up and *appreciate* her new take on ultra-conservatism, and get it through his thick head that she knew the difference between fantasy and reality.

Catherine threw herself into the fray and it wasn't long before she was tackling the 'home run'—the top drawers of Max's ten ancient filing cabinets. The oldest, mustiest files. And they were hard to reach for someone who was only five feet four.

She was standing on an upturned wastepaper basket when the accident happened.

She'd tugged one of the drawers open, hands buried blindly in it to extract the first few files, when the wastepaper basket slid out from under her. She fell backwards, pulling one file with her and scattering papers in an airbound muddle. The filing drawer, tugged along by the force of Catherine's other flailing hand, slid fully out, disengaged from the cabinet and started a heavy descent to the floor.

'Cathy?'

She heard Max's herald from the lift lobby as she hit the floor almost simultaneously with the drawer, which landed next to her as she let out a mangled *ouhmph* sound.

Winded. *Great!* How was she supposed to look ultra-conservative lying on a carpet of loose pages, gasping for breath, next to a filing drawer?

Well, the filing alcove was tucked away. Hopefully Max would think she'd left the office on some errand and go into his own office. She could wait out the diaphragm spasms in peace, then get up, straighten her clothes, and walk back to her desk as though nothing had happened.

'Cathy?' he called again, obviously having reached her desk and found her missing.

Catherine closed her eyes. Two minutes was all she needed. *Go into your office,* she begged silently. *Two minutes, that's all. Two—*

'Cathy?'

By this time Max was sounding puzzled, irritated, and a little alarmed.

*Oooohhh*, this was *not* going to work.

'Catherine North! Where the hell *are* you?'

Followed by a string of graphic curses.

She willed her diaphragm into submission and managed to draw an uncomplicated breath. One more. A third.

Right. Time to get up—so she could at least be found on her feet.

But she'd only managed to raise herself on one elbow when Max hurtled past the open door of the filing alcove. Stopped. Turned. Charged back, another string of curses accompanying him.

Catherine raised herself on her other elbow. 'No wonder you wanted the files cleared out,' she said, with only a faint wheeze. 'They're a health hazard.'

'I'll tell you what you can do with the files,' Max ground out. Kicking loose pages out of his way, he shoved the errant drawer aside with such ferocity that Catherine hoped he'd refrain from filling her in on the intricacies of that particular suggestion.

In seconds he was kneeling beside her. 'What happened? Should I call an ambulance? I'll call an ambulance.'

'You will *not* call an ambulance,' Catherine said. 'Because I'm fine.'

'You're not,' Max contradicted flatly. 'You didn't answer when I called. Did you hit your head?'

'Yes, but—'

Without waiting for the rest, Max delved one of his hands

into her hair and Catherine groaned. There went her tight chignon; she could feel waves of hair springing out all over the place.

All it took was the groan for him to dig deeper. 'There? Does it hurt there?'

'No, it doesn't hurt there,' Catherine said waspishly. She reached a hand up to her head. 'Oh, what are you doing to my hair? Do you know how long that takes to pin?'

'So don't pin it,' Max said. He got to his feet, effortlessly drawing Catherine up beside him, then put his arm around her. 'My office,' he said, and started shepherding her along.

Catherine groaned again. This was too awful. Not only the embarrassment of being discovered in such an undignified position, but the fact that Max had his arm around her, so she was breathing in that erotic scent of his—that mixture of special cologne, ultra-clean clothes, and Max's own personal essence. At close range it was too wonderful to be borne.

'I'm fine, I promise you,' she said feebly.

'Nearly there,' Max soothed, shouldering open his office door, settling her on the leather couch against the wall, crouching beside her. 'All right, now just lie there.'

Catherine would have preferred one of the matching chairs where she normally sat. A couch was so…intimate. It reminded her of an Alex-Jennifer scene—Jennifer reclining on a chaise-longue, hair tumbling over her shoulders; Alex staring down at her with burning eyes…

Max smoothed a hand across the top of her head and Catherine groaned again.

'See?' Max said accusingly. 'You *are* hurt!'

'Oh, for goodness' sake,' Catherine grumbled and, using her hands for leverage, tried to sit up.

'Look,' Max demanded, grasping the hands pushing against the leather of the couch and lowering her again. 'You're shaking like a leaf.'

It was true. And Catherine was very glad to have the fall as an excuse—because her body's trembling reaction had nothing to do with that fall and everything to do with Max's proximity to her.

'All right, a headache and a teensy bit of shock,' she lied. 'Now, can I get up?'

Max squashed himself onto the edge of the couch beside her and put his hand to her forehead—feeling her temperature, of all things. Well, he *was* an engineer, not a doctor.

'I guess that's a no,' Catherine said dryly. 'Although I think you should consider doing a first-aid course.'

'I thought I was managing pretty well.'

'*Hmph.* It's a good thing I didn't injure my back, the way you dragged me off the floor.'

'What—was I supposed to leave you there?'

'And I don't have a fever, so you can move your hand.' Next thing he'd be asking her to stick out her tongue—and there was no saying what she'd do with it once it was out of her mouth!

Max removed his hand. 'How am I supposed to know if I don't check?'

'Because you don't get a fever from—' Catherine broke off in exasperation. 'Oh, never mind! Just tell me when you're free for that first-aid course.'

'Why didn't you answer when I called?'

'I was flat-out at the time.'

The bone-melting smile. 'A *double entendre*—so your brain's working at least. Are you sure you didn't break anything? Perhaps I'd better check—'

'If you do, I'll walk out of this office and never come back.' Just to *think* of those hands wandering over her bones was enough to heat her blood to boiling point.

'All right, all right.' Short laugh. 'God, you're such a firebrand, Cathy. I love it.'

*Firebrand.* Catherine's breath jammed. Jennifer was the firebrand. Catherine wrote her that way because she couldn't be like that herself any more, not since RJ... *Uh-oh.* Not a good idea to be thinking about RJ. Or *Passion Flower*. Or tongues. Or fires in the blood.

'Stay there,' Max commanded, standing in one smooth, decisive movement. 'Five minutes.'

But it was less than three minutes later when Max returned, a glass of water in one hand and two tablets in the other.

'For your headache,' he explained, and watched as Catherine downed them. 'Now,' he said when she'd finished her last swallow of water. 'Explain.'

Catherine looked at him blankly. 'Explain what?'

'What the hell you were doing.' He passed a hand that was none too steady over his eyes.

*Whaaaat?*

'I was doing the filing. As requested by *my boss*.'

'I didn't mean for you to kill yourself!'

'And I didn't.'

'Couldn't you get someone else to get the files for you if they were too high?' He started pacing in front of her. 'In fact, why *are* they so high?'

'I have no idea. I guess your last assistant was taller.'

'Elise,' Max said, matter-of-fact. 'Yes, I guess she was.' He looked at Catherine's feet, her hideous flat shoes. 'She wore high heels, too.'

'Well, it seems your various *Elises*—' oozed Catherine, dripping poisoned honey '—never threw out a piece of paper in their lives! I've found files so old they should be given a gold watch!'

'Do you need help going through them?' Max asked, ignoring her sarcasm to cut straight to the point.

Instantly Catherine's back was up. *No way* was she going to get landed with a leggy blonde 'Elise' to help her. 'I'm nearly finished. I can handle it.'

Max looked at her sceptically.

'I can,' she insisted.

Max was silent, studying her for a long moment. Then he got to his feet and walked over to look out of the window. 'So…how's the book going?'

Catherine pokered up. 'If you think that's the reason I haven't finished—'

'That's not what I—' Max broke off, spinning around. 'I just...had an idea. You know...for a scene. I thought of it while I was in Queensland.'

Catherine opened her mouth to tell him to mind his own damned business—but for some reason out came, 'A scene?' instead. Because—*arrggghhh*!—she was interested. Intrigued, even. And clearly insane.

In. Sane.

'Yeah. A cocktail function where Alex is trying to woo investors,' he said. 'Jennifer has planned the event. And something goes wrong. She...she twists her ankle or...or hits her head, maybe...? And Alex has to rescue her, and he calls the doctor and...and stuff.'

'What kind of party? I mean, black tie?' Catherine frowned, thoughtful. 'Because Jennifer doesn't dress up.'

He hurried over to her, sat on the edge of the couch again. 'This could be the first time she does though, couldn't it? And he's thinking, *Wow, who knew?*'

She stared at him, her brain ticking over. 'Hmm... Maybe I could try that.'

His eyes were so warm, so serious. For a heart-stopping moment Catherine thought he was going to touch her. She flinched backwards and Max jumped to his feet.

'I just wondered, that's all,' he said, and paced to the other side of the room, jamming his hands under his armpits. 'That's how he'd treat her, right? Alex? How he'd be with Jennifer if she needed help?'

Okay, maybe she had a concussion and Max had some bizarre kind of interstate-travel version of jet lag. Because there was no rational explanation for this conversation.

'I think I should get back to work.'

Max unjammed his hands, shoving them into his hair instead. 'Not until the doctor has a look at you,' he said, and all but ripped the phone off his desk. 'I'll call him, then go and bring Damian up to speed. Give you some privacy while the doc's here.'

Alex…calling the doctor. Max…calling the doctor. This was weird. *Too* weird.

Catherine was so fidgety she could barely respond to the doctor's questions. And when she was pronounced fit and well and was back at her desk with the filing she couldn't concentrate. Because whenever she saw Max's bold hand-writing on a document she'd remember how it had felt to have his arm around her, his hands in her hair, that look of worry creasing his forehead and darkening his eyes, him talking to her about *Passion Flower*.

*That's how he'd treat her, right? Alex. How he'd be with Jennifer if she needed help?*

Yes, that was exactly how he'd be.

And it had triggered other *Passion Flower* scenes, which now started rolling in her head. Sex in the filing alcove. Sex on the couch in his office. Sex on her desk—after Alex had wiped the top clear of all distractions…vicious staplers, hapless rulers, all flying off.

When she found herself mixing up the 'keep' and 'archive' files for the fourth time she started digging her *own* hands into her hair, even though it was back in its nice tight chignon.

And that was when she started really worrying—that she could write romance novels until the cows came home and still not get her feelings under control.

This was *not* going to turn out well.

When Max started reading from the top of page one for the fourth time he finally gave up.

He shouldn't have touched Catherine. At all. Let alone going the full Neanderthal, dragging her off the floor and digging his hands into her hair. But now he *had* touched her he wanted to touch her again. Really, *really* wanted to. Like drag-her-close, breathe-her-in, put-his-tongue-somewhere touch her.

He shoved his hands into his hair and tugged. The truth was he'd wanted to touch her forever. Even when he hadn't understood why.

And then, that night when they'd worked late, it had started to make sense: his brain had been seeing under her skin, where his eyes didn't reach, and everything under there had been slowly but surely reeling him in. The sharp-as-a-tack brain. How she giggled to herself when she thought he wasn't looking, making him wonder what was funny and why it was secret. Her stalwart defence of misfits like Carl—who'd better not have been sniffing around in his absence! The volcanic eruption when they disagreed on something, followed almost immediately with the grab for her top button or her earlobe—even though she had to know she didn't have to be nervous around him; she could say anything to him.

In Canada, he'd convinced himself that their partnership was not to be screwed with because she was the best assistant he'd ever had. Which meant hands-off. But then he'd come home and she'd been sitting there in that tight top with her hair loose—and he'd known his hormones had been in on the act with his brain all along, seeing what his eyes hadn't. The total, outrageous hotness of her.

Well, a fat lot of good his hormones had done him! Because she'd dressed like that for that day's anonymous lunch companion—not for *him*! She only ever treated *him* to starchy buttoned-up shirts and shapeless drab skirts. No wayward curls for Max's viewing. No sexy black tops. No alluring red silk peignoirs.

Peignoir... Max groaned and gripped his head, two-handed.

That book!

The second tactical error he'd made today. *Why* had he asked her about Alex and Jennifer? What sort of coward's way was *that* of finding out how Catherine wanted to be treated by a man? And what difference would it make if he *did* know how Catherine wanted to be treated when she didn't want *him* to be that man?

Damn Alex Taylor, anyway.

Alex. Black hair. Six feet two. Italian leather shoes. Navy leather couches. A view of the Botanic Gardens.

*Arrggghh!* Everything fitted—whether the eyes were blue or amber or pink!

Why *couldn't* Alex be him?

He opened the report again and did his best to read past the first paragraph. But it was no use. Within thirty seconds the report was languishing, unloved, on the desk.

She'd ruined him—that was what she'd done!

She had him ignoring the steady stream of leggy blondes all clamouring for his attention. Had him running away from his own office to get his raging passions under control. Had him becoming his own personal assistant because he was too scared to take her on perfectly legitimate business trips.

Well, this state of affairs could not continue.

He was experienced with women. Successful in business. A shrewd entrepreneur used to getting his own way. A natural and efficient problem-solver.

One frosty-pants spinster was *not* going to get the better of him.

It was time to take control.

Time to kick things up a notch and see what happened.

Yep, it was time to fix this...this *travesty*.

Word of the day: 'travesty'.

What his sex life had become.

# CHAPTER FOUR

WHEN CATHERINE ARRIVED at work the next morning she was amazed to find that the old filing cabinets had been replaced by ones that were shorter, sturdier and safer.

She barely had time to marvel at the change before the second miracle of the day happened: Nell showing up with two clerical assistants to help transfer the files.

'Care to swap bosses?' Nell asked. 'Somehow I can't see Damian commandeering staff to make a job easier on *me*.'

'Max *commandeered* you?'

'He told Damian you'd had an accident with the old cabinets and he was making sure it didn't happen again.'

'But it won't happen again with these new ones,' Catherine said. 'And I don't need help. So I'm grateful, but—'

She stopped suddenly. Because she could *smell* him.

'I see your help has arrived.'

Max.

Catherine turned towards the doorway of the filing alcove where her boss—supremely indifferent to Nell and the two assistants at half-swoon—was leaning against the doorjamb.

He was wearing a navy blue suit, the whitest of white shirts and a gold and navy silk tie, and had somehow managed to get more handsome overnight.

'Yes,' Catherine said, past a sudden tightness in her throat. 'And thank you for arranging it, but there's no need—'

'No more buts—I have no intention of listening to them. In fact, I really hate the word "but". Why not "okay" or "of course" or "I'm fine with that"? There's way too much butt-ing.' He was about to breeze out again when he seemed to have second thoughts. 'And, Cathy—you're here to direct—not to do the work yourself. I want you to take it easy after that bump on the head yesterday.'

'But—'

'*But.* Tsk-tsk-tsk. Not liking that word.'

Nell sighed as he left. '*Please* swap bosses,' she begged. 'I'll *pay* you!'

Three hours later the job was finished, but for a small num-ber of confidential files Catherine had insisted on looking after herself, and Catherine was alone in the filing alcove.

She opened the necessary drawer, quickly sorting through folders until she reached the section she wanted. She put the files away, pulled out one that had been misplaced—

And then the unmistakable scent of Max filled her nos-trils again.

*Give me a break!*

She turned quickly, landing a file-carrying wallop to Max's ribcage.

He stepped away, rubbing his ribs. 'Ow! What did I do?'

'You sneaked up on me,' Catherine snapped—which she figured was more acceptable than, *You smell too good.*

'I didn't sneak.'

Catherine turned back to the filing cabinet, put the file in the correct place.

'What's got up your nose, Cathy?' he asked the back of her head.

*Nose. Scent. You. No!*

'If you must know it's embarrassing, having people trucked in to help me with work I can easily do myself.' She reefed open another drawer.

It was like viewing an erotic movie, seeing Max's hand moving in front of her to close the drawer. Long, lean fin-gers. Clean, square, no-nonsense fingernails. Tanned skin. White cuff.

Longing flooded her belly as her heart started that familiar slam against her ribs. He didn't touch her, and she didn't turn to face him...yet she felt him in every pore.

'Catherine,' he said, and she felt goosebumps rise all over her at the softness of his voice. 'What's wrong?'

*Swallow. Boss. Work. Real world.*

'I just don't want to be the subject of office gossip. I mean about...about you doing things...special things...for me.'

'There is nothing gossip-worthy in getting you some help with the filing after that accident. If Damian had asked for you to be released to help Nell under similar circumstances I would have agreed in a heartbeat.'

Heartbeat. Heart. Beat. Her heart. Beating too heavily.

She said nothing, just kept her eyes on the filing cabinet in front of her.

'The only thing gossip-worthy in this office is your book,' he continued. 'And the fact that the hero bears a striking resemblance—'

'I told you he's—'

'—to me. And unless you've been showing *Passion Flower* around—'

'Of course I—'

'—there isn't a problem.' Pause. 'You're like Rutherford Property's Miss Lemon—all efficient and fastidious and incorruptible.' Pause. 'I mean...*Passion Flower* aside...aren't you?'

Another pause, during which Catherine kept her eyes on the filing cabinet, completely incapable of forming a word.

'Aren't you, Cathy?' he asked again. 'Take *Passion Flower* out of the equation and nobody would believe we were having a steamy affair even if they caught us walking around together naked.' Pause. 'Would they?'

Catherine screwed her eyes shut. Of *course* nobody at Rutherford Property would think staid Ms North was capable of a sexual thought, let alone an affair. Just as no man would ever fantasise about her—*least* of all her drop-dead-gorgeous boss.

Which was exactly the way she wanted it.

So she had no business—no business at all—thinking of Alex and Jennifer in the filing alcove, Alex spinning Jennifer to face him, leaning her back against the filing cabinet. *'Let them gossip,'* Alex would whisper. *'I don't care. Just kiss me.'*

Catherine's hands were damp. Her lungs were joining forces with her tripping heart and refusing to stick to a normal physiological pattern. Her body was one big throb.

This was unbearable.

She bolted her eyes open and quickly pulled out a new drawer, even though she had nothing left to do. She flicked a few files around for no reason.

'You might want to stand back,' she said. 'I don't want to hit you again. Accidentally.' *Or on purpose.*

But Max didn't move. 'Why would anyone be gossiping, Cathy?' he asked again.

A little more purposeless file-fiddling. 'They wouldn't. You're right. I overreacted because I just like my space.'

Max stepped back. But there was no time for even a quick mental *whew* because he sighed, and she felt it on the back of her neck—the problem with chignons was that they left your skin bare there—and her legs almost buckled.

'There's something else,' he said. 'You're stewing over something. I know you.'

*Yes, I'm stewing over you and my need to jump your bones.*

Hmm, perhaps not. She stared at her perfect files, trying to come up with an answer. Files. Neat. Perfect.

*Bingo.*

Catherine slammed the drawer shut and turned to face Max. 'All right. I'll tell you. I've been wondering if there's something about my work you're unhappy with.'

'Huh?'

'My work. Do you have a problem with it? I mean, aside from not liking my filing.'

'Huh?'

'Because there was no other reason to get three extra people in today. And you've been away on two separate trips in the past month and have barely communicated with me except through Damian. That's not reassuring.'

'No, I don't have a problem with your *work*,' he said, as though she were insane. 'You're perfect—as ever.'

*'Perfect—as ever.'* Alex could say that to Jennifer in the filing scene as he reached for the buttons on her shirt. *'But let's muss you up a little.'*

God—enough with *Passion Flower* already.

Catherine produced a perfunctory smile that just touched her pinched-in lips. 'Then, if you'll excuse me, I'd like to check that everything is fine in here before I go to lunch.'

'No, I won't excuse you,' Max said. 'I want you in my office now.'

'I said I'd like to—'

'Do I have to play the boss card, Catherine?' he asked, cutting her off.

'But—'

'Ah, that word. The boss card it is, then. Catherine—I said I want you in my office. Now.'

He turned on his heel and Catherine was left fuming. The boss card. Things would be better all round if he would stick to playing the boss card *all* the time. Maybe then she would stop being distracted by how criminally hot he was.

She cruised into Max's office as regally as the *QEII* and remained standing, all rigid dignity, wasting a witheringly astringent look on Max, who was sitting behind his desk and didn't even bother to look up.

A minute passed.

'For God's sake, get off your high horse and sit down on that nice *navy leather chair*, Cathy,' he said eventually—but he still didn't bother to look up.

*Oooohhhh!* She really wished she could force-feed him every page in *Passion Flower* that mentioned those damned chairs, then ask him to repeat 'navy leather chair' with a giant wad of paper stuck down his throat!

But with a small touch of her gold hoop earring she sat, as stiff and upright as a ramrod. And waited, waited, waited. Max jotted notes in the margins of a document. Set that aside and picked up a report. Started reading, every now and then dragging a hand through his dishevelled hair.

*Hello? You dragged me in here to watch you mess up your hair?*

She cleared her throat—trying to redirect his attention to where it should be. On her!

Max looked up. 'Do you need a glass of water?' he asked, the solicitousness of his voice at odds with the challenge in his narrowed eyes.

'No, Mr Rutherford, I do not need a glass of water,' Catherine said, and despite her righteous irritation her hand leapt defensively, protectively, to the button at her neck.

'Max,' he corrected automatically. Then he lowered his head again, muttering something Catherine couldn't hear.

She waited, seething. There would be no 'Max' today. Not if she had to stick her mouth on the binding machine and thermo-seal her lips shut!

And then, abruptly, he looked up again. 'The filing is finished?'

'Yes.'

'So are you ready to ditch the bitter and twisted now? Nell needed to learn the system—that's the other reason I had her help you today.'

She could feel her nostrils flaring. 'Damian keeps his files separately.'

'Nell is about to start looking after this office as well,' Max said.

'I don't underst—'

'It's quite simple,' he interrupted. 'I've arranged with Damian for Nell to keep the office—*my* office—in order.'

Catherine's blood froze. 'Are you telling me my services are no longer required?'

'Huh?'

'I thought you said my work was perfect?'

'It is.'

'Then why? Is it—is it about my book?'

'I'm more than happy to talk about your book, Cathy, believe me—but what the hell does it have to do with Queensland? Unless… Are you putting that scene in? The cocktail party?'

'Yes—yes, I am.'

His eyes lit. 'Really?'

'Yes, it's…good. It's…' But she was too distracted to think clearly and finish that. 'So…you're not sacking me?'

Max stared at her for a moment, and then he laughed. 'Do you *want* me to sack you? Because you ask about it every second day! The answer, for the next twenty times you ask, is no. I'm not sacking you. I'm just taking you to Queensland.'

'Queensland?'

'We'll be away for a week.'

'We?'

'Yes—we.' Max favoured her with a fierce glare. 'We—as in you and me. No—you and I.' Hands in hair. 'Oh, you know what I mean.'

'I'm afraid I don't.'

Max shot her a look of pained patience. 'It's quite simple. I'm needed in Queensland for a series of meetings about Kurrangii. Everyone involved—the bankers, the solicitors, the architects, the lobbyists, the PR and marketing teams—will be there at some stage over the next week, so it makes sense to work from there rather than fly back and forth every day. And, frankly, I'm tired of being my own assistant when I travel. You said you wanted to be busier, and you know the project inside out, so you're coming with me.'

Max yanked open his desk drawer and pulled out a few sheets of paper, stapled together. He leapt from his chair, stormed around to her and waggled the document under her nose.

'Take this.'

Catherine took it, stunned to see it was a copy of her job description. Max had gone over two parts in hot pink highlighter pen: *'Must be available to travel'* and *'Required to act as hostess for extracurricular events on occasion'.*

'Well?' Max demanded.

'It's my job description.'

'Yep.'

'But...the travel... You've never needed me with you before.'

'I'm not in favour of disrupting the lives of my staff if I can avoid it. I can no longer avoid it.'

'Okay, fine.'

'Fine? So...that's it?' He looked wary. 'You'll come?'

'Yes, of course.' Aside from the fact that Catherine was so relieved she still had her job she would have flown to Pluto, it made perfect sense for her to accompany him.

And in any case it was her favourite project.

And it would be a wonderful opportunity to see her brother, Luke, who'd relocated to Port Douglas a year ago.

And, if she were honest with herself, another week in the office without Max might just tip her into lunacy.

'Do you have definite dates?' she asked. 'I'll make the bookings straight away.'

'I've done it,' he said cautiously. And then made a faux scared face as he saw her reaction. 'Uh-oh—the death stare!'

'I do not have a death stare.'

'Oh, you *so* do!' he said, and laughed.

Catherine had to basically choke herself from the inside to stop laughing, too.

'Go on—laugh,' Max said. 'Dare you.'

She pinched her lips in. 'It's not funny.'

He looked at her for a long moment and then, with a shrug, strode back behind his desk. He picked up the report again, flipped through it.

'There's a lot happening in Queensland. Not only the meetings, but business dinners and a cocktail reception. The local team has managed the basics, but I want you to do the finessing. I know you have experience with that kind of stuff. I mean, from your last job with the airline—Samawi Air, right?'

Catherine stiffened. She had to make a conscious effort to answer evenly. 'Yes, I managed events there.'

'I know that was in the Middle East, so I'm guessing very conservative…?'

'Actually, I managed events for the airline globally, including Australia. Nothing in Queensland will be a problem.'

'Oh,' he said, with a doubtful look at her. 'It's a *luxury* airline, right?'

'Yes. It's only small, and not well known, but it is a luxury airline,' she said, knowing he was getting at something. It wasn't like him not to just spit out what was bothering him. 'Why?'

'I just…' Long pause. His hands were in his hair. Out. In. Out. And then he took a visible breath. The way you did before diving into a deep pool. 'I've made arrangements for you to visit a boutique this afternoon.'

Catherine's mouth dropped open. She wondered for a moment if she'd misheard.

But, no.

Because Max made an exasperated sound and said, 'A boutique. You know what a boutique is, don't you?'

He ran a discerning eye over her body, making her screamingly aware of the unattractiveness of her white shirt and tan wool skirt.

'No, maybe you don't…'

And the fact that he said that last bit to himself was *not* a comfort.

Her mouth snapped shut and her fingers reached for her shirt button as she took the insult on board. She reminded herself that her disguise was all about keeping her straight on the fact that work was work—signalling to *Max* that work was work. So nobody had to worry about fending off sexual advances. And it was obviously working brilliantly. Just *brilliantly*! She should be pleased. *Very* pleased.

Instead she was so furious she could have leapt across the desk and ripped his hair out.

'It's on my account—all arranged,' Max said. 'So don't worry about the money.'

Catherine sucked in a sharp breath. 'I don't need new clothes,' she said carefully.

Max rose a second time from his chair, walked over to Catherine and plucked the job description from her hands. '"Required to act as hostess for extracurricular events on occasion",' he read, and then looked at her over the top of the page. 'One of the terms under which you accepted your position with Rutherford Property, right?'

'Yes, but—'

Max held up his hand. 'I am getting *so* tired of that word. No *buts*, Catherine.'

He went back to his desk, scribbled a name and address on a piece of paper and held it aloft.

White-lipped, Catherine stood, came forward, and snatched the proffered paper.

'We're building an upmarket resort—*way* upmarket,' Max said. 'I don't want anyone associated with the project to look like they've just checked out of a thirty-nine-dollar-a-night motel. This applies to every meeting, and it applies absolutely to the cocktail function, where we'll need to wow potential investors—including the top executives from global airlines, hotel groups, tour companies. We all need to look the part or how can we be expected to sell it?'

'Is that all?' Catherine heard the tremor of rage in her voice but couldn't seem to control it.

Max peered at her, right into her eyes, starting to look a little uncertain.

Catherine lifted a hand to her spectacles. No doubt he was going to suggest designer frames. Or contact lenses. And why stop there? Why not get some contacts that made her eyes violet or blue or green?

But with an awkward shrug Max lowered his eyes and wrenched his mobile phone off the desk. 'I'll call Sandra—

she owns the boutique—and brief her on the type of things you'll need.'

As Max started scrolling through his phone for the number Catherine digested the fact that Max was obviously on very good terms with Sandra (said as Saaandra, of course) and wondered how many other women she'd dressed for him. The thought of being one in a long line made her want to throw something at his head. Something sharp. Like a spear.

'I'm sure you're *very* well acquainted with women's clothing,' she said, allowing herself just the one dig.

Max didn't bother to look up. 'I know enough to do the choosing if Sandra isn't satisfied with what you buy.'

Catherine very precisely folded the piece of paper Max had given her. 'I'll go now, then, shall I?'

Max nodded.

'And *you* can go straight to hell,' she said under her breath as she sailed out of the office.

# CHAPTER FIVE

THAT NIGHT CATHERINE said aloud the name of the tall, blonde—surprise surprise!—*'Saaaaaaaaaandra'* with each item she removed from the shopping bags, relishing adding an extra 'a' each time until she felt as if she was gargling it. Gargling—and spitting!

She was *so* furious! She was even furious that she was furious!

But she couldn't help it.

The last time she'd been on a work-related shopping spree had been for her final Samawi Air event. A VIP dinner in Washington, D.C., celebrating the airline's inaugural flight to America. She'd been so buzzed because it was the biggest event she'd ever been involved with and she'd worked incredibly hard to make it perfect. RJ had forced her to accept a clothing allowance—a *'legitimate business expense'*, he'd said—to ensure she looked perfect, too. Even though in those days she'd dressed beautifully, always, by both instinct and inclination.

So she'd bought a new dress—and wowed RJ so spectacularly he'd all but ripped it off her. She'd ended up wearing an inconspicuous suit to the dinner, her glamorous hairdo replaced with a tight bun, any pride or pleasure she'd taken in the job gone.

She shivered, remembering how powerless she'd felt that night. How sickened, and shattered, and enraged, and impotent. And...*scared*. Scared for the first time in her life.

But that had been then; this was now. A totally different set of circumstances.

If she hadn't spent the past four and a half months dressing so deliberately badly Max wouldn't have had to roll out the company credit card. He simply had no idea she already had a wardrobe bulging with possibilities. And Max's brief to 'Saaaaaaaandra' had been clear: conservative, classy, stylish. There was nothing sexy or provocative about the clothes selected for her. No reason to feel like a call-girl being outfitted by her pimp. Nothing to trigger a bodice-ripping free-for-all.

So why were those same feelings of shame and distress and anger and fear infiltrating her common sense as she looked at them? Why was she stuffing them back into their bags? Why was she pulling out woollen skirts, boring shirts and cardigans, low-heeled pumps and thick tights to pack instead?

All the rage suddenly left Catherine and she slumped onto the bed. She knew why she was packing her 'grandma' clothes. She didn't want to risk inciting another man to attack her because of the way she looked. It was about safety—*not* a word that had figured heavily in her vocabulary in the pre-RJ days, but one that seemed to dominate her life now.

She saw her future, stretching ahead. The rest of her twenties, thirties, forties, fifties… Dressing as a ninety-year-old at the office but wearing a peignoir in secret at home, to remind her that she hadn't *always* been 'Miss Lemon'. *Pathetic.*

Her doorbell rang and she sighed. It would be her neighbour Rick, who forgot his key so regularly she'd offered to keep a spare for him. He was always so jovial she'd get depressed just looking at him! She glanced down at her peignoir and managed a small laugh. There would be no 'inciting' going on in this get-up. Her biker's leathers would be a different story!

She hurried to the entrance hall, dug Rick's key out of the dish on the console table and opened the door—and squealed with joy! Her brother, Luke, was standing there, holding a bottle. She threw her arms around him.

'Careful, Cath, the wine's Grange,' Luke said. 'I thought you could drink me under the table in style this time.'

Catherine tugged him inside and closed the door. 'What are you doing in Sydney?' And then she looked at him in sudden dismay, said again, 'Sydney?' and punched him in the arm.

'Um, Sydney, yeah...' He rubbed his arm.

'Yes—you're in Sydney, and I'm flying up your way tomorrow! I was going to surprise you. Why are you here?'

'I'm down for a book-signing—standard stuff. But what's *your* deal?'

'Work. One week. Travelling with the boss. We're building a luxury resort in the Daintree Rainforest. When are you heading home?'

'Monday.'

Catherine relieved him of the wine. 'Great! We have a night off on Wednesday.'

'Book me in.'

'But tonight...' She smiled. 'I have a new chapter for you to read. Stop groaning! It won't kill you to give me some advice.'

It wasn't until they were settled on Catherine's well-stuffed two-seater couch, wine glasses in hand, manuscript pages on the coffee table, that Catherine remembered she wasn't dressed for visitors. She cast a rueful glance at her peignoir. Okay for handing Rick his key, but a little boudoir-ish for entertaining her brother.

'One of the best things about family,' Luke commented, catching her eye, 'is I couldn't care less what you're wearing.'

'It's just a fancy dressing gown, really. But I should have dragged something a little less burlesque over the top before opening the door.'

'Why? There are no rude bits showing or I already would have ordered you off to change.' He looked searchingly at her face. 'But on the subject of covering up—are you still playing dress-up at work?'

'Afraid so.'

Luke's eyes narrowed, his whole body tensing. 'The new boss. He hasn't tried anything?'

Catherine laughed, a little forlornly. 'I'm not his type. He's so hot he's boiling. His last assistant actually chased him around the desk! By comparison, today he told me I'm the Miss Lemon of Rutherford Property.' She sipped, sighed.

Luke stared at her. 'Was that a *sigh*? Tell me you haven't done anything as mundane as falling in love with the boss?'

'It's not *love*.'

'Not *love*—but it *is* something? Crikey—*you're* not chasing him around the desk, are you?'

'Now, that *would* be mundane, since it's already been done.' Catherine grinned at him. 'But the Dance of the Seven Veils has crossed my mind.'

Luke choked on his wine.

'He'd put the veils back on me, though. Quick-smart.' Another sigh. 'You know, Luke, I don't make sense—even to myself. Dressing like I do to make sure my boss doesn't touch me—and yet somehow…*wanting* him to. What's wrong with me?'

'Nothing. Not one thing. You're just…testing the boundaries, maybe? Or perhaps your subconscious is giving you a nudge, telling you it's time to think about escaping that gaol you've built around yourself, but you're not *quite* ready to open the door. And it's not about how hot your new boss is, or how hot or cold you are, either. It's about trust. Do you trust him, Cath?'

'Yes, absolutely. I know—*know*—it's not in Max to force himself on anyone. Even aside from the fact that he has women throwing themselves at him. But…' Quick breath. 'But what if RJ was right? What if it was what I did, how I acted, the way I looked, that made him do those things? What if I change my look, or do or say something now, with

Max, and the things I want to happen do happen—and then I find I don't want them to happen after all?'

'Then you say stop. And if your boss is who you think he is he will.' He looked at her, very serious. 'What RJ said is what bottom-feeders say to justify themselves. You did nothing wrong, Cath. You have nothing to reproach yourself with—no reason to feel guilt or shame.'

She felt tears prickle and blinked hard. 'There *is* shame, Luke. Because I ran away and I let him get away with it. And it makes me so *angry* with myself. I'm so angry...so often.'

'You couldn't have done it any differently.'

She shrugged restlessly. 'Anyway, let's not talk about it. It will spoil our evening.'

'Maybe we haven't talked about it *enough*.' He took her hand, squeezed. 'Cath?'

Pause. Uncomfortable.

And then Catherine shrugged again, moving her hand out from under his. 'No, I'm good. And as for Max... Well, Max is nothing like RJ. I have no need to worry.'

Luke sighed.

'Please, Luke. Not tonight.'

'All right.' Quick, unhappy smile. 'So, if Max is nothing like RJ, when is Catherine-the-Great coming out to play and putting Miss...Miss Lemon, is it?...back in the box?'

'Catherine-the-Great is already playing. In *Passion Flower*.'

'Where it's nice and safe because you can live vicariously and remain in complete control of who does what to whom.'

'Hey—some of my scenes are a little out of control, you know! There's a scene on the boss's desk that would make even your jaded eyes bug out.'

'The boss's desk...' Luke gave her a long, musing look. 'You know, I wonder if your boss sees more than you think? I have a theory that you can only hide your true self for three months and then the real you will leap out waving a flag, yelling, "It's me! I'm back!" Nothing you can do to stop it.'

'Well, I'm past *four* months at Rutherford Property—and counting. And I promise you the only thing my boss sees when he looks at me is my granny clothes.'

'I thought you said he was smart?'

'He is. Very.'

'Then he's twigged to the real you by now.'

Catherine thought about Max's occasional piercing looks. His intermittent curious comments and questions and digs. The way he'd recognised her so quickly in *Passion Flower*...

Except that he hadn't really recognised her in *Passion Flower*—not the essence of her, only the hair, eye colour and glasses—or he couldn't have called her Miss Lemon.

'No, Luke. He actually sent me off for fashion advice today, so I don't disgrace the firm on this trip. Don't laugh—it's true!'

'Oka-ay...' he said, but didn't sound convinced. 'So... the book? No chance of turning it into a murder mystery?'

'Why? Are the hearts and flowers really going to freak you out? I won't force you to read it if they are.'

'It's not the hearts and flowers I object to—it's the sex scenes. *Yeeeuuuch!*'

'What's wrong with them?'

'Well, to start with you're my *sister.*'

Catherine laughed. 'I'll weed out the sex parts before I hand over the pages, okay?'

'Hit me!' he said, and took a fortifying gulp of wine.

The wine had been consumed, pages of Catherine's manuscript were scattered across the carpeted floor and Luke was preparing to depart when the doorbell rang again.

Catherine looked at her watch. 'Wow, it's almost ten-thirty.'

'Who are you expecting?'

'It'll be Rick from next door. I have his spare key. This will only take a second.'

Catherine hurried over to dig in the dish on the hall table for a second time and opened the door, smiling—and the key slipped from her fingers right along with the smile from her face.

Max Rutherford was standing there.

Just like a scene she'd written for *Passion Flower*. Alex turning up at Jennifer's house, all hard-faced and intent.

And in Max's case, stunned as well, as he looked at her hair.

Then his eyes dropped to her peignoir. 'Huh,' he said, and swallowed.

Luke made an unhelpful strangled sound and Max's eyes shot straight to him.

Smiling easily, Luke walked over to them, and Catherine managed to get over her shock long enough to string an introduction together. 'Luke Phillips, this is Max Rutherford—my boss. Max, this is…is Luke. I've mentioned him *before*.' Nice and pointed.

*Alex Taylor, at your service.*

Max said a clipped hello to Luke, then returned his eyes to their previous target: Catherine's peignoir. A few scorching seconds and then his gaze roamed behind her, to the living room. Catherine got the feeling he was processing a different element of the scene with each small movement of his head, his eyes.

She felt an almost overpowering urge to explain Luke's presence, the peignoir, the wine, the book—but she gritted her teeth to stop herself, because it was none of his business.

'Is there a problem, Max?' she asked, and if there was a touch of defiance in there, too bad!

Max's intent blue stare returned to her, wandering over her face and up to her hair. Catherine reached a self-conscious hand up. Her hair was loose, tumbling.

Instead of answering, Max looked at Luke again.

'I'm just leaving,' Luke said hurriedly, 'so don't let me get in your way—unless—' he tugged at a hank of Catherine's hair '—you want help clearing up. Or you need me to find those veils…? Seven, right? Seven veils?'

'No need for those tonight,' Catherine said, and gave him

a too-hard hug that promised violence at a future date. 'So I won't keep you—but thanks for your help with…you know.'

'Any time. So I'll see you…soon?'

'Yes, soon,' Catherine agreed.

Luke cast a way too interested glance at Max as he bade him goodnight. Then, with a jaunty whistle, he left.

Catherine stood there, tongue-tied, waiting for Max to speak.

'Did I interrupt something?' he asked at last.

'No.'

More silence. A heavy silence she didn't know how to break. Because she had no intention of babbling an explanation about Luke being her brother—well, half-brother—and a novelist, and telling him that he'd been giving her advice on the book she was *never discussing with Max again.*

Max smiled, but it didn't reach his eyes. 'I told you today I wanted to cause as little interruption to the lives of my staff as possible. If taking you away for a week is going to be a problem for anyone—you know, *anyone*—I can rethink it.'

She stared at him while that sank in. *Oh. My God.* Luke was going to laugh himself sick when she told him Max thought he was her boyfriend. Not that the existence of a boyfriend was a valid reason to skip Queensland, anyway— but it was just so brilliantly ridiculous!

Catherine clamped down on a give-away giggle and said ambiguously, 'I don't let my private life interfere with work.'

'Seriously. I can easily take someone else. Nell, for example. If you need to stay in Sydney. For any reason. You know, any reason. At all.'

He was *fishing*! For information on Luke!

*Insaaaaane.*

'It's not necessary,' she assured Max, very breezy and unforthcoming.

'No…no encumbrances, then?'

'Nothing that will interfere with this trip.' She thought it best not to add that in fact she would annihilate whoever got in the way. Nell. Max. Anyone along the flight path between Sydney and Cairns.

Max looked at her for one long moment. 'All right, then.'

'All right, then,' she repeated.

Then…nothing.

The house was deathly quiet, as if it was waiting for something.

She could smell Max's cologne and it was making her want to lick him—right under his ear, where a tiny kiss curl of black hair sat against his skin.

She moved fractionally, nervously, towards the door—a hint for Max to state his business and go before the temptation got too much for her. Felt the faint swish of her silk sleeve brushing Max's arm. Heard his sharp intake of breath. Now she'd taken that step they were standing way too close to each other, and it was excruciatingly good.

Why didn't he just take the hint and leave? But he didn't budge.

'Hot,' he said.

*What the hell…?*

He gave his head a tiny shake. 'In the city,' he added. 'It's hot in the city. Tonight, I mean.'

*Whaaat?*

'Oh. The…the song?'

'No.' He shook his head again, as if to clear it. 'Nothing.' Pause.

Catherine took another small step towards the door.

'Your hair looks nice,' Max said.

'Thank you,' Catherine managed to get out of a suddenly dry throat.

He touched her hair. Just a fleeting touch. 'Why do you always pull it back in a bun?'

A strange liquid warmth was invading her limbs, making them feel heavy. 'It gets in the way. I mean, for work.'

'I see.'

Silence again. Thick. Impenetrable. She could hear her own breathing, and it wasn't sounding normal.

Giving no indication of an imminent departure, Max walked into the living room—as though he had a perfect right to wander around her house. Typical Max! He looked at her furniture. Narrowed his eyes at the wine bottle. Frowned at the haphazardly strewn manuscript pages, staring as though he'd absorb every piece of print on them.

Catherine was paralysed by a strange push-pull desire— to move closer to him and at the same time run upstairs, lock herself in the bathroom and shove cotton wool up her nostrils so she could stop smelling him.

She took a panicky breath. 'So, what—? I mean why—? I mean... *Is* there a problem?'

The silence had stretched to snapping point but Max didn't seem to care. He bent to pick up some pages, started speed-reading.

*God!* She hurried over, wanting to rip the pages out of his hand.

But when she got there he pointed to a paragraph and said, 'You know, this part's been bothering me.' He dropped the pages. 'The angle.' He took Catherine by the shoulders, and positioned her in front of him. 'Alex is six-two, right?'

*Swallow. Nod.*

'And she's...what...? About your height?'

*Nod. Biiiiig swallow.*

'So when he takes her in his arms like this...'

He had pulled her into his chest. She was going to faint. *Help! Help, help, help!*

'...and he holds her, like this...'

*Oh. My. God.* One of his hands was in her hair, the other on her lower back.

'Well, can you see where her head should be?' he asked, but he didn't sound like Max. 'To do what you've written he'd have to...'

He had his hand under her chin, was lifting her face to his, staring at her mouth. Something was going to happen. Something momentous. Did she want it to? She didn't know. Could hardly breathe.

'Have to...?' she asked, all quivery.

But before Max could answer the doorbell rang—again—and Catherine wrenched herself back to earth and out of his arms.

She stood there, staring at him.

*Doorbell. Ringing.*

She blinked, blushed—and ran to answer it, hearing Max's muffled curse. Thank God for whoever was out there. Because she wasn't ready for...for...whatever *that* had been. She'd welcome anyone. Dracula. Mr Hyde. Freddy Krueger.

But this time it *was* Rick—who looked monster-scary, with his shaved head and his vicious-looking tattoos down each arm, but who was gentle as a lamb.

'I know I'm hopeless, South,' he said. 'Sorry!'

Catherine looked blankly down at her hands, then remembered she'd dropped the key and bent to locate it and pick it up. She held it out to Rick, who grabbed her to give her a quick kiss on the cheek before snatching it.

'Angel! How's the book travelling? Have you added in a bit more sex, like I suggested?'

A quick, nervous look over her shoulder at Max, to find him watching her, looking a little serial-killerish himself. 'Luke says less sex—you say more!'

'Luke likes cold, dead bodies; I like live, warm ones. I'd say that makes *me* the normal one.'

'You have a point.'

'And remember what I said—I'm available for research purposes. But not if you're wearing *that*, South.'

And then he was gone, and Catherine turned to find Max striding towards her with blood in his eye.

'So, we've had Luke lolling around like a sultan drinking wine. Rick flinging around nicknames and kisses. And me. How many more men have you got dropping by to offer you some raw material?' he exploded. 'And don't tell me it's none of my business!'

'Well, it's not,' Catherine assured him, wrapping her peignoir a little more securely.

Max grabbed her, and this time there was no gentle instruction about where her head should be. Just a wrench into his arms.

'I'm making it my business,' he said.

# CHAPTER SIX

MAX STARED INTO her eyes. One split second. All heat and furious energy and unleashed lust.

And then his mouth was on hers.

*Oh. My. G-o-o-o-o-d.*

It was nothing like the soft kiss she'd imagined for Alex and Jennifer in *Passion Flower*. This was desperate and straining. *Un*imaginable. His mouth fusing to hers, devouring. Tongue searching, filling her. He tasted so…so *hot*. No, hot wasn't a flavour. She tried to concentrate, to isolate the taste, but then one of his hands was in her hair, and then both his hands were there, delving, burrowing, tugging to angle her head for his mouth, and she *couldn't* concentrate.

A burst of fire was rocketing through her core, crackling along her veins. Where were her hands? Her arms? She had no idea. Couldn't think. All she could do was stand there, anchored to Max by his hands in her hair. Better than her fantasy. Max claiming her. Max wanting her. She could *feel* him, big and hard against her. His hands were moving again, circling her neck, his fingers warm, stroking. But never, not once, did he disengage his hungry mouth from hers.

Catherine wanted to open her eyelids, see him, imprint this on her brain, but she couldn't seem to move them.

'Cathy…' he murmured against her lips. 'Cathy, I want—' But he didn't finish that. Simply kissed her again, thumbs at her jaw, tilting her face, kissing her, kissing her as though he couldn't help himself.

And then, very suddenly, he stopped. Let her go. Jerked back.

Catherine's eyelids managed to flutter open as her wondering fingers came up to press against her tingling lips. The last time she'd been kissed it had been RJ—harried and frightening and disgusting. Nothing like this...this *magic*. She didn't want to lose the feeling. Wanted a moment to savour it before reality came rushing back. So she held her fingers there, as though they could contain the taste of him, the feel of his mouth.

He gave a shaky half-laugh. 'So now I know,' he said.

'Now you know what?' Catherine asked through her trembling fingers.

'That I'm not Alex Taylor. Well, *that* sucks!'

She blinked. 'That...sucks?'

Max ran his hands agitatedly into his hair. 'You told me I wasn't, but I didn't believe you, and now... Well, now I guess I do. I'm not Alex and you're not Jennifer.' Pause. One shoulder hunched. 'At least you're not *my* Jennifer.'

Catherine's fingers dropped. She was momentarily bereft of speech. Of all the things he could have said he'd said...*that*?

'So you kissed me just to prove a point about my *book*?' Catherine asked when she could find her voice.

'I didn't plan on kissing you, Cathy, it just happened. Like—like my blood suddenly boiled.' Another one of those shaky half-laughs. 'Where are the vampires when you need a blood-letting?'

'Well, Max,' Catherine said, dangerously calm, 'if you'd care to bring your jugular vein into the kitchen I'll grab a carving knife—in the absence of fangs, you understand.'

That startled him. 'Huh?'

'I'd be delighted to drain your blood,' she said, and saw the *aha* moment hit him.

'Uh-oh, the death stare,' he said. 'I said something wrong, didn't I?'

Catherine pursed her lips. 'Oh, I don't know... Do you mean the part about preferring to be attacked by a vampire

to kissing me? Or the part insinuating I was a lousy kisser—
*unlike* the heroine in my book?'

'But I didn't mean— That's not what I—'

'So what will it be?' Catherine interrupted. 'A severed
jugular vein? Or will you leave my house immediately and
never come near me again? I'll accept either option.'

'Enough with the death stare, already,' he said, grimacing.
'I kissed you, you said no thanks—no harm done.'

She'd said *no thanks*? She shook her head, dazed. *Un.
Believable.* 'You know what? Keep your blood. Less mess
for me to clean up if I just resign.'

*He* shook *his* head. 'Again with the sacking thing?'

'Not sacking—resigning.'

'Well, you're not resigning. I need you.'

'Oh, I'm replaceable.'

'No, you're not.'

'Perhaps with a nice tall blonde you actually might *want*
to kiss.'

'No! It's not— It's not *you*, Cathy, it's—'

'Puh-leeeeease,' Catherine interrupted, with a massive
eye-roll. 'Let's not do the "it's not you, it's me" routine. I'm
well aware I'm not your type. *"Nobody would believe we
were having a steamy affair even if they caught us walking
around together naked."* That's right, isn't it?'

'But I didn't mean—'

'No buts, remember? And, whatever you want to say, it's
a moot point—because *I resign.*'

He looked mulish now. 'Well, I'm not accepting your resignation, so get over it.' Hands in his hair again. 'Look—
does it help if I say I'm sorry I kissed you tonight?'

'You've made that abundantly clear.'

'Will you shut up and listen? This is not about *me* not enjoying it. It's about *you* not enjoying it. *That's* how I know
I'm not Alex Taylor. Because you didn't kiss me back. If
you'd kissed me back I would have swept you up in my arms
and whisked you off to bed and we'd be having a *very* different conversation now.'

Okay—that stopped her. 'But I...' Stop. Swallow. 'I *did* kiss you back.'

'I've kissed a lot of women, Cathy. A *lot*. I know the difference between *being* kissed *by* someone and being *allowed* to kiss someone. I haven't had someone "allow" me to kiss them since I was fifteen. Summer. School gym. Sian Michaelson. It was like kissing a block of wood. Rare—therefore memorable.'

'A block of *wood*?'

Blinking. Stunned. Mortified.

But Max had leap-frogged ahead. 'So the question is, why did you let me? It's not like you to let anyone take liberties.'

'It just— You just—' She broke off. How did you explain such a thing? *Every woman on the planet wants to kiss you, Max, why would you think I'm any different?* Um—*no*! Not after being likened to block-of-wood Sian Michaelson.

He was watching her, eagle-eyed. 'It just— I just— What?'

'Look, since it was so unmemorable let's forget it happened.'

'It wasn't unmemorable.'

'Oh, yeah—memorable for its woodenness, right? A mistake, then.'

'Mistake?'

'You said it was a mistake.'

'No, I didn't.'

'You said you hadn't planned to kiss me.'

'Actually, I *had* planned to. Just not tonight.'

Not *tonight*? But he *had* planned to...? What the *hell* was going on?

Catherine couldn't find her voice.

'So?' he asked, head on one side in curious mode.

'So what?' Cathy replied. Flustered.

'Well, it happened. So now what?'

'We—we forget it.'

'Forget it? Hmm...'

'Put it down to a fleeting attraction now satisfied.'

'But I'm *not* satisfied. And you *certainly* weren't. I'm

going to have to up my game before you'll let me try again, aren't I?'

'A *fleeting* attraction,' she reiterated, drawing his attention to the salient part.

'Fleeting? Hmm...'

She rolled her eyes. 'Anyway, a fleeting attraction. And because this is a weird situation you lost your head.'

'What's weird about it?'

'Okay, your losing your head is not that weird. But you being in my *house* is. As in not being in the office. And I'm wearing this red thing—which I shouldn't be wearing.'

'Why shouldn't you be wearing it?'

She stared at him. 'Um—because look what *happened*! I mean, come on—personal assistants shouldn't sashay around like this—' she plucked at the silk '—in front of their bosses.'

'You let me kiss you because you *deserved* it for flaunting yourself at your boss in red silk? Is that what you're saying? That's insane.' He laughed, as though it really were funny.

Catherine's eyes dropped to Max's chest and stuck there.

'Cathy, you *cannot* be serious.'

'It's not funny, Max.'

'It kind of is.' Pause. Sigh. 'Are you going to look at me some time soon, Cathy, do you think?'

Up came her eyes, but it wasn't easy. 'There. Now what?'

He shrugged, a smile lurking. 'I've got no idea. You'll have to tell me, because I've never been in this situation before.'

That got a scoff out of her. 'Oh, really? Never kissed your personal assistant before?'

'Never kissed a woman who didn't *want* to be kissed,' he clarified. 'Even Sian, back in the day, wanted me to lay one on her. I didn't have to force her. She just didn't know how.' He paused, an arrested expression on his face. 'Is *that* the problem? Inexperience?'

She gave him a withering look. 'I'm not inexperienced.'

'Well, that's what I think when you start talking about

sashaying in front of your boss wearing a peignoir. Hello, Queen Victoria.'

Her temper spiked. 'I'm not a virgin, you know.'

'How *would* I know? You look like one! You *act* like one. Want to prove to me that you're not?'

'What—? How—? I— *Ohh!* Just because I'm not some hot blonde—'

'Well, not *blonde*, at any rate.'

'—it doesn't mean I'm de-sexed.' Quick furious breath. 'I know enough to identify the difference between a *mutual* kiss and having one *forced* on me at any rate. Because I've been there!'

Max had been opening his smiling mouth to say something else, but that stopped him. Flat. His eyes zoomed to hers. Sharpened. Focused.

'You know the difference…' he said, and Catherine could practically see his brain working. Tick, tick, tick. 'Okay, it's not funny any more. Who was it? When? What happened?'

Catherine was furious with herself. Her damned temper! 'Forget it. It's nothing.'

'If you think I'm going to forget that, Cathy, you've got boulders in the brain.'

'I don't want to talk about it. I've been *trying* to forget it. I am *not* going to relive it. Okay?'

He paced away from her, then back. Away. Back. Dipped his head, looked into her pupils. Long, hard stare that had her holding her breath. And then he said, 'Oh, my God,' as though he could see everything.

He closed his eyes and stood like that for a long moment.

And everything felt…different. Tense…awful. Even the air felt as if it had been replaced with something heavier, thicker, darker.

'M-Max…?' she said, suddenly off-kilter.

He opened his eyes, looking utterly appalled. 'So now you've had two bosses force themselves on you.'

'No, I've had *one*,' she said. 'You *didn't* force yourself on me because that kiss was *mutual*. You are nothing like that—that—'

*Stop. Regroup. Calm down.*

'I wouldn't be working for you if you were anything like him. You are nothing like him. *Nothing*.'

And wasn't *that* becoming more obvious with every passing second? RJ would have had his hands all over her by now. He'd have been coercing her, then threatening her. Max, by contrast, looked as if he was going to make a dash for the carving knife she'd threatened him with earlier and slash his *own* throat—over a kiss she'd been dreaming of for months.

Time to get back to basics. 'I'm not bringing a sexual harassment suit against you, if that's what's worrying you,' she said.

He stared at her as though he couldn't believe what he'd just heard. 'That's not what's worrying me, Catherine. *I'm* what's worrying me. What I did to you.' Hands in his hair. 'You should have slugged me. Next time just take a shot. In fact, take one now. Slug me one.'

'I'm not taking a *shot*.'

'I'd feel better if you did.'

'And I'd feel worse.'

And somehow, suddenly, the words were just…*there*. Tumbling out.

'Of course if you do something like…like making a time for me to come to your hotel room to discuss a work problem… then answering the door wearing nothing but a towel…then locking the door and dropping the towel…and trying to make me come over and pick it up…I'll slug you then.'

*'What?'*

'Or if you sidle up to me at a staff party and complain about the erection I've given you just by being there—one so *gigantic* you can't get up and make your speech—and then you grab my hand and force me to feel the evidence— then I'll slug you.'

'I—*God*!'

'And if you and Damian ever share a disgusting, filthy

smirk because Damian comes into your office while you've got me backed against the wall, trying to put your hand up my skirt while I'm trying to get away... Yep, I'll slug you.'

'Catherine—'

'But I'm not slugging you for a kiss I *wanted*.' She realised her whole body was trembling. 'And now I need to sit down.'

'Let me help you.'

'I can walk to my own couch!'

He cleared his throat. 'I want to help you.'

She stared at him, shook her head in disbelief. 'Don't tell me you, of all people, have a Sir Galahad complex!'

'Ha-ha,' he said, and pulled her quite roughly under his arm. 'Come here and shut up.'

Okay, that was typical Max! Impatient, pretending to be bad-tempered, just because he cared and was embarrassed to show it. She was about to talk about the most hideous episode in her entire life—something she didn't even discuss with Luke—and because Max had said exactly that, pulled her in just like that, somehow it felt...*right*.

So she let him lead her to the couch. Let him plump the cushions. It reminded her of how he'd coddled her after her fall in the filing alcove.

When the couch was prepared to Max's satisfaction he gestured for Catherine to sit. 'Can I get you something?' he asked, all gruff. 'Water? Booze?'

'What—are you the homeowner and I'm the guest?' she asked, choking on an unexpected laugh. 'No? Then come here and shut up.'

He laughed as he sat beside her. And then he patted her hand. God, there would be a lap rug and a crochet pattern coming her way soon.

'Are you okay?'

'Yes, Sir Galahad, I am okay.'

'So...do I need to kill him for you?' Said as though he was just going to pop out for a coffee.

*Oooohhhh...* How could you *not* fantasise about such a man?

'He—my ex-boss, RJ Harrow—would say it was all my fault,' she said. 'So why should *he* be punished?'

'All your...?' Max was looking horror-struck. Too horror-struck to finish that.

'And I have to say that at the very least I was guilty of criminal naivety, because it took me a few months to notice... Well, nothing concrete. Just a...a feeling. A few grandiose compliments but with a certain look when he gave them. Too many checks of my computer screen over my shoulder. An accidental nudge in the corridor a little too often. All explainable. But then it moved on to other things. A shoulder massage while I was typing, even though I asked him not to. Hello and goodbye hugs which were almost...unbreakable. And things kept escalating and escalating, and...well...'

She paused, yanked her hair back, rolled it tightly into a bun and reached for the pen on the coffee table.

'The final straw happened in Washington, D.C.,' she continued, shoving the pen through the bun. 'I was in charge of organising an important dinner for VIPs, media and corporate customers. Warned that everything had to be perfect—including me. So RJ gave me a clothing allowance.'

Max leapt to his feet and started pacing, as though he had too much energy to keep still.

'Shall I stop?' Catherine asked.

'No! No, I just— No. Keep going.'

'Well...I was so anxious about everything being perfect that when he called me to complain about the mess I'd made of the seating plan, demanding I come to his hotel room to sort it out, I ran straight there.'

She winced, remembering how clueless she'd been.

'But it was just a ruse to get me alone and off-balance. Because the seating plan was perfect. And so, apparently, was I, in the new dress *he'd* paid for.'

Pause. She hated this part.

'So of course RJ couldn't be expected to resist me. That's what he said. My fault for looking like that. And he kissed

me so hard he split my lip. He had his hands— His hands—
He tried to—' Another pause. 'He tore that dress right down
the front in the struggle. But at least I got away—more or
less unmolested.' She gave Max a strained smile. 'And that
was the end of my career at Samawi Air.'

Max's pacing had come to a stop. 'The clothes,' he said.
'I bought you clothes—like he did.'

'It's different.'

'I kissed you against your will.'

'That wasn't against my will. I *wanted* it to happen.'

He started that edgy pacing again. 'You didn't even touch
me, let alone kiss me. Not once. *I* did all the touching.'

Catherine blinked at him. *All* the touching? Max had done
it *all*? No. No, she wouldn't believe that.

'It was mutual,' she insisted.

'You don't need to do your "there, there" routine with
me—patting my head and kissing it better.' He winced. '*Ugh.*
Wrong choice of words.'

'No, kissing is the *right* choice,' Catherine said. She
jumped to her feet, walked over to Max. 'Let's settle it.
Kiss me again. I'll kiss you back. Then we'll know.'

He stared at her as though she was insane. 'I'm not kissing you again. It's bad enough I crossed the line once.' His
hands went digging into his hair. 'Hell, I didn't cross it. I
somersaulted over it!'

'You're not *that* good a kisser.' Which was a lie, but someone had to ratchet back the hyperbole. 'Let's call it a toe
nudging the line.'

At least that seemed to sting him out of the doldrums,
because he said with a slight huff, 'If I'm not that good, why
would you want me to kiss you again?'

Catherine shrugged...very casual. 'To prove a point.'

'It will ruin things.'

'Things are already ruined. So, come on—pucker up.'

'No. We'd be better off forgetting tonight ever happened.'

Which was what *she'd* originally suggested, of course,

but it hadn't suited him at the time! Well, it was too damned late now. A woman didn't get called a block of wood—and a virgin at twenty-six years old—then turn up for work with no hard feelings.

Catherine suddenly didn't care about crossed lines. She was somersaulting over the line *herself*—with three twists, a tuck *and* a swivel!

She fixed Max with a steady eye. 'I wasn't going to tell you this—your ego is massive enough already—but Luke is not Alex Taylor. Damian, Carl, Rick—nope. You are. Just you. Alex Taylor.' She drew herself up, very grand. '*Now* what do you say?'

'Nice try.' He shook his head. 'I know the way you operate, Cathy—all psychological and kind if someone is having a hard time. It's one of the things I love—' He stopped, cleared his throat. 'Well, one of the things. But I don't need to kiss you again to know you didn't kiss me back the first time. So don't worry. I won't overstep the line again.'

Catherine threw her hands in the air and spun away from him with an inarticulate half-scream of frustration. They were going round and round in circles.

'So, Catherine—your call. What happens next?' Max said, and she spun back to face him.

She opened her mouth to say, *Kiss me—that's my call,* but Max was already rolling right along. Typical!

'Maybe you'd prefer to work for one of the others. Only...' Pause, frown, shake of the head. 'I don't think Damian is the right fit for you. And Carl... Well, Carl...no. Just no. Get that thought out of your head. But of course if you *want* to go to one of them...'

Yep, he was making a lot of sense!

'Or, on the other hand, if you *want* to stay working with me,' he continued, as though he hadn't just banned her from going to one of the others, 'we can play it by ear, make sure you're comfortable. But skip Queensland, obviously. I'll send a courier in the morning to pick up the clothes from

Sandra's. I can't believe I—' He stopped, ran a hand over his eyes. 'Anyway, take the week to think about what you'd prefer, and I'll accommodate whatever option you want.'

If Catherine knew one thing it was that she was *not* skipping Queensland. Max's modus operandi for dealing with mistakes was to lop the experience off like a dead tree limb and spread fertiliser on a new plant. Well, she was not giving him time to lop her off. And if any plant was going to be fertilised it was going to be her!

Drastic action required, obviously. 'So you're punishing me for what *you* did?'

'What? No! I just don't want you to be uncomfortable. I just— Dammit, Cathy, of course I'm not punishing you. I'm trying to look after your interests.'

'You said you'd accommodate any option I chose. Well, that's the one I'm choosing. You know, it could be considered passive-aggressive behaviour to take this opportunity away from me. Now I think of it, all those trips you've been taking lately, sending messages for me through Damian—passive aggressive. Textbook. Are you trying to get me to resign?'

'I only— I mean, I was doing that because—' He broke off. Sighed. Twice.

Oh, my God, he was so *adorable*. Confused, bemused, bossy, earnest, controlling, tortured, with absolutely no idea how desperately she wanted to throw herself at him. At this point, however, he'd probably have a coronary.

'Just tell me I can still go to Queensland,' Catherine said.

She didn't want to have to take things up a notch and guilt-trip him with a few tears, but she'd do it if she had to. Because she was not—*not!*—going to sit in the office for a week, imagining Max entertaining a parade of blonde bimbos while having an occasional piece of typing lobbed at her via Damian. Not after tonight.

'Okay.' Max sounded goaded past bearing. 'But if you change your mind at any time just say the word. If I say something stupid that makes you uncomfortable just tell me, okay? Because I will. Say something stupid. I know that much about myself.'

'I promise to tell you if you say something stupid, the way I always do, because you are always saying something stupid. You've said a lot of stupid things already tonight.'

'Yeah, maybe with a little less alacrity,' he said, his un-accustomed hair shirt slipping off one shoulder.

'All right. Less alacrity when I'm pointing out that you're being an idiot. The way you are now.'

He looked as if he was going to snap, and she waited hopefully, but he got it under control. And Catherine had a sinking feeling that 'control' was going to be his middle name from now on.

Ruined! Completely. If he'd kissed every inch of her three times over and whisked her off for an all-night orgy with his favourite sports team things couldn't have been more ruined.

'Okay, I'm going,' he said. 'Just don't worry.'

'I'm not worried,' Catherine assured him.

He headed for the door, looking suicidal, and Catherine hurried after him.

'Did you hear me? I'm not worried!'

He opened the door, stopped. Turned to her, very grave. 'Catherine, we don't need to talk about it again. But just to tie everything off: I was at fault—not you; it won't happen again, and we'll get things back to normal.'

'Things were never normal,' she pointed out.

His lips tightened. 'All right, back to *ab*normal,' he said through his teeth. 'Just don't worry.'

'I'm not worried!' she said again, nice and loud and ex-asperated.

But the words bounced off the door that Max had quietly closed.

He was gone.

'Well, that went well,' Catherine said aloud.

And then she kicked the door.

\* \* \*

Max got sedately into his Alfa Romeo Spider. Very calm, in control.

Then he banged his head against the leather-covered steering wheel. Twice. Hard.

All he'd intended to do tonight was drive by and, if he saw Catherine's light on, drop in and check everything was on track for Sunday, that she didn't need a ride to the airport.

Okay, that was a lie!

What he'd really wanted was to see if she wore a red peignoir at home—like Jennifer. And she did. If she let her magnificent hair down at home. And she did.

So, with those boxes ticked, what had he done? Crashed down on her like an avalanche of testosterone. As though the hair and red silk were a trigger. *Boom!*

Okay, that was another lie.

He'd wanted to kiss the breath right out of her for the past two days, when she'd been more starched up and pinned in than ever before—without a peignoir or a loose curl in sight! And she'd tasted so good, felt so lovely, it had taken him too long to notice she wasn't being transported like he was.

Which had shaken him; he wasn't used to non-transported women. That had to be the reason he'd started babbling about Alex, Jennifer, vampires. Vampires, for God's sake! But it hadn't stopped him wanting to take another bite of the cherry. Hadn't stopped him calculating how to make it better, hotter, irresistible—so she'd *have* to respond next time.

All that flirty conversation, hoping to make her laugh the way he knew she always wanted to, sussing out his chances of being given another try. Even going so far as to ask her if she wanted to prove to him she wasn't a virgin. *Grooooooooaaaan!* He deserved to be lobotomised for that!

And then—the unravelling.

He could still feel that drop in the pit of his stomach when she'd told him what had happened to her. The impotent fury of hearing how her bastard ex-boss had shifted the blame to her. The revulsion of understanding the link between that and Catherine blaming herself for tonight's kiss. Because of what she was wearing, because she was 'sashaying', like some devious *femme fatale* intent on getting her hooks in him. Her fault—not his, *hers*.

Way to make him feel like…like his father.

He scrubbed his hands over his face. His father, the infamous Flip Rutherford, played his own blame-game in order to indulge himself with an endless conga line of secretarial sex partners.

*'She had that look in her eye…' 'She dressed a certain way…' 'She's got a track record with her bosses…' 'Looking like that, of course it was going to happen…'*

Pathetic excuses.

Like Max's own excuse—*Passion Flower.* Cathy was Jennifer and he was Alex—she must want him like crazy to have written that book, so why not take what was offered?

Except that it hadn't been offered; he'd just taken.

Max sighed heavily. How had he got to this, anyway? Hunting Catherine North. *Agonising* over Catherine North! She wasn't even his type. She wasn't blonde. She wasn't tall. She wasn't beautiful.

At that point in his deliberations Max banged his head on the steering wheel again. Not beautiful? Try telling *that* to the thing in his pants that kept straining towards her like a divining rod lunging for the mother lode.

Well, it was just going to have to work out how to *un*strain itself. Because he would be an absolute monster to touch her again now he knew what had happened to her.

How was he supposed to even interact with her? Carefully, he guessed. Honourably. And he was hardly the careful, honourable type.

He looked in the rearview mirror. 'You are not going to so much as breathe on Catherine. Got it?'

His face stared back at him, looking mutinous.

God, if his *face* wouldn't behave how was he going to control the rest of his body?

One week in Queensland, with the hottest woman on

the planet, and he couldn't touch her. Could a man suffer a stroke from a sustained, unrelieved hard-on? Because that was going to be him!

One serving of misery, coming right up.

'Misery': word of the day.

Catherine was one of the first passengers on board the aircraft on Sunday morning. Spectacles gleaming, nondescript navy skirt creaseless, fully-buttoned white shirt accusingly crisp, grey cardigan forbiddingly neat, work folders on her lap.

A very deliberate look—and stage one of her plan of attack.

She'd figured that appearing completely unfazed by what had happened on Friday night, in her regular uptight persona, would stop Max reaching for the cat o' nine tails and whipping himself the moment he saw her. She was not going to let gung-ho Max even *think* about grabbing an instrument of self-torture, because once he did he wouldn't easily relinquish it.

She only hoped he hadn't been self-flagellating all of yesterday! Because if she had to trade brilliant, brusque, politically incorrect, challenging Max for hair-shirt-wearing Max, walking on eggshells around poor sexually harassed Catherine, she might just kill him.

She *hated* being poor, sexually harassed Catherine! She was so *over* poor, sexually harassed Catherine. She would not *be* poor, sexually harassed Catherine for one more second.

Which brought her to stage two of her plan: she was going to seduce her boss.

First—because she wanted to.

Second—to prove she was not a block of wood.

And third—because it would mark her liberation from RJ Harrow.

She was turning the tables, breaking out of gaol. *She* was going to be the one stalking and pouncing and getting her rocks off. And they'd see what Max thought of poor little, harassed Catherine who couldn't kiss back after she'd banged his chivalrous brains right out of his head!

But, given Max's Sir Galahad complex, she figured she was going to have to seduce by stealth—so he wouldn't know what had hit him until it was too late for him to shore up his defences. It would have to be done piece by infinitesimal piece, one hairpin at a time.

And she had a suitcase full of ammunition for the battle.

After *Saaaandra*'s clothes had been collected on Saturday morning Catherine had determinedly searched through her own clothes—her *old* clothes, her *beautiful* clothes. She'd gone for just over the edge of modest. Except for the shimmering red evening gown, which was *waaaaay* over the edge of modest and heading towards dangerous. Because *that* was for the cocktail party—the night she was going to get Max Rutherford into bed.

She took a deep breath at that point, because her insides were out of control and she needed to be cool, calm and collected for her first interaction with Max.

She suspected he'd be the last passenger on board—partly because that was typical Max, and partly to spare her his company for as long as he could.

Living up to her expectations, Max hurricaned onto the aircraft just before the doors closed, striding to his seat as though it were everyone's duty to wait for him. He was wearing a lightweight chocolate-brown suit and a shirt in palest lemon—no tie. His hair was its usual bed-head style. It was such a good look she committed it to memory for Alex Taylor.

'Good morning,' Max said, with a smile that managed to be both friendly and a little remote.

But Catherine didn't miss the tiny flicker of relief that crossed his face as he noted her attire. *Ha!* He'd better not get too used to that!

Catherine smiled back, nice and uptight, to lull him further into a false sense of security. 'Good morning,' she said, and then paused, just for a nanosecond, before adding, 'Max.'

His eyes widened, and with a slight air of desperation he plucked the in-flight magazine from the seat pocket in front of him and started riffling through the pages.

Catherine concentrated on breathing in the smell of him, drinking in the sight of his long, strong fingers flipping the pages. Was the air between them vibrating or was that just her imagination? Well, regardless, Jennifer Andrews was going to join the mile-high club. And perhaps, on the way back to Sydney, so was Catherine North.

Max turned towards her to point out an article on the Daintree Rainforest, and Catherine—heart-rate trembling—instinctively grabbed for the top button of her shirt.

'Don't worry, it's done up—you're safe,' Max assured her, and then immediately found something on the other side of the aircraft he just *had* to look at.

Damn—she had to stop grabbing for that button! Well, she would fix that.

'Actually,' she said blithely, 'I was going to *un*button it.'

Max's head snapped back fast enough to give *her* whip-lash.

She undid the button, all innocence. 'It's a little…hot… in here, don't you think?'

Max said nothing.

So she popped a second button. Saw his tiny swallow.

And then he said, 'Safety demonstration,' and turned to watch the flight attendant, apparently completely absorbed.

But Catherine wasn't giving up. She waited for the safety demonstration to conclude, then said calmly, '*I* need saving, actually.'

Another whiplash turn. 'Huh?'

She handed over a folder.

Max opened it, and she heard his breath being sucked in. 'What are you doing?' he asked.

'Don't you know what that is? Friday night, remember?'

'Yes.' Very dry. 'I *do* remember Friday night, as it happens.'

'It's the scene from *Passion Flower*. The one you said

wasn't working. I rewrote it. I think it's greatly improved, but I need your input. Your being six feet two and all. You know the scene? When Alex takes Jennifer in his arms... what goes where...how they feel...the way he—?'

'So one moment I'm not allowed to see the book and the next I am?'

'So one moment you're dying to see the book and the next you won't look at it?'

She saw the struggle on his face. And then—very suddenly—he retrieved his briefcase from beneath the seat in front of him and shoved the folder inside.

'If this is some kind of test it's not necessary, Cathy.' He looked at her then. 'I'm not going to read it and then ravish you. You're safe with me.'

Safe. Just when she wanted to be in danger.

*Safe.*

Catherine reached for the in-flight magazine, blinking furiously, wondering why she was so close to tears now when she hadn't cried—not once—during the whole RJ debacle.

*Six nights,* she chanted to herself, staring blindly at a photo of a beach. In six nights she would be fluttering like a butterfly, no matter how hard Max fought to keep her protected in the chrysalis she'd so stupidly made for herself.

It was past time to say goodbye to Miss Lemon and welcome back to Catherine-the-Great.

Catherine had gnashed her teeth hard enough to wear off the enamel by the time the flight landed in Cairns.

She'd undone a third shirt button: no response. Refastened all three: no response. Pretended to be thrown by a sudden aircraft movement so her arm ended up in Max's space—not that a grey-wool-clad arm was particularly seductive, but you had to use what you had available. No response.

She'd been racking her brain for a few other experimental moves suitable for implementation in an aircraft cabin when Max had resolutely donned his headphones and turned on his in-seat entertainment system—and she'd had to admit defeat.

At the baggage carousel, Catherine thought of and discarded a dozen conversational gambits—but it wouldn't have mattered if she'd hit on the most brilliant topic of discussion ever. Because Max didn't give her an opening. He was ignoring her without actually ignoring her. Quite a skill! He chatted about the weather, what they'd see on the drive, how long it would take—blah-blah, boring blah—until their driver located them, their baggage was bundled onto a trolley and they were heading towards the exit.

He was going to be a tough nut to crack.

And then, as they stepped out of the airport and into the almost suffocating moist heat of Cairns, two things happened one after the other: a tall, gorgeous, leggy blonde, wearing an exquisite lilac mini, bowled up and kissed Max on the cheek and Catherine's glasses fogged over.

'Darcy, glad you could make it to the airport,' Max said, with the merest flicker of an eyelid towards Catherine, who was willing her glasses to acclimatise quickly to the humidity so she could properly gauge the competition. 'We can talk contracts on the drive. Let me introduce you to my assistant, Catherine North. Catherine, this is Darcy Appleby, the lead solicitor on the Kurrangii project.'

'Oh, Catherine, your *glasses*!' Darcy exclaimed.

The annoying, tinkling, laugh that accompanied that made Catherine want to slap her.

'Max, you'll have to give her some of your shaving cream. Rubbing them with that should stop the fogging.'

Catherine chose not to answer. Because into her head had popped an image of Max shaving while a naked Darcy hovered behind him. Then, through the open bathroom door, a crazed killer materialised, wielding a meat cleaver...

'And I hope you brought some cooler clothes,' Darcy said, interrupting her own imminent demise, 'because this climate is merciless.'

Catherine looked down at herself, even though she knew very well that she was *not* wearing a lilac mini and gorgeous caramel high-heeled sandals, but a too-hot navy wool skirt,

low-heeled black pumps, a boring white shirt and that goddamned cardigan.

'I have it all under control,' she said. And replaced the
meat cleaver in her mind with a nice big axe.

Yep, Queensland had got off to a fabulous start.

# CHAPTER SEVEN

THE DRIVE TOOK a little over an hour, and it was murder—which was obviously the word of the day.

Catherine sat in the front with the driver, Darcy in the back seat with Max, indulging in a long discussion with him that finished with, 'Everything will be ironed out by Friday, Maxie-T!' accompanied by that annoying laugh.

*Maxie-T?* Catherine couldn't stop her eyes rolling. And, really, she didn't try. Maxie-T? Seriously?

'Excellent,' said Max, not telling Darcy to can the idiotic nickname the way any sane man would.

'Do you want me to act as hostess for the cocktail party like last time?' Darcy asked.

*Last time?* Catherine's teeth were clenched so tightly the hinges of her jaw throbbed.

'No need,' Max said. 'Catherine's got that under control.'

'Catherine?' said Darcy, aghast. 'Oh, you mean, she's organised a professional event hostess?'

*She?* Oooooohhhhhh… *'She'* was sitting with a perfectly working brain and tongue in the front seat, able to think and speak for herself!

Catherine's nostrils flared so dramatically it was a wonder her septum didn't snap under the pressure.

'Who's she hired?' Darcy asked Max, just as Catherine pictured the bathroom killer wielding the meat cleaver in one hand and the axe in the other. Yep—two-handed. It worked for her. Maybe an ice pick between the teeth, too…

'No, I mean Catherine's the hostess,' Max said, answering for her.

*Helloooooooo?* Not invisible. Sitting in the same car. Functioning brain *and* voice-box. With serial killer wielding multiple instruments of death in head.

There was a moment of stunned silence from the back seat, then Darcy moved on to another subject.

For the sake of her mental health Catherine tried to tune out their conversation and concentrate on the view through the windshield—mountains on one side, coast almost close enough to touch on the other.

Failed spectacularly.

At one point Max leaned forward to tell Catherine they were approaching Port Douglas and a rush of liquid heat hit her square between her legs. She had to clamp her thighs together. He said something about the Great Barrier Reef, and Catherine—an uncomfortable mix of aroused and livid—worked on ignoring him. She even managed a huffy toss of her head. Which didn't really signal the dismissive irritation of having her solitude interrupted the way she'd hoped because her hair was in such a tight bun.

Not that Max noticed it, anyway. When she failed to reply in actual words he simply returned his attention to the bimbo. Okay, she wasn't a bimbo—but still!

By the time the car turned off for Moss Falls Retreat, Catherine's bloodbath psycho-killer scene was playing on a continuous loop in her head.

They pulled up at the resort and there was flurry of activity as staff came out to take bags and proffer keys. Then the flurry died down and Max turned to Catherine, smiling in that newly remote way she *hated*!

'Take the rest of the day, Cathy—it's Sunday, after all. Look around, relax, have a swim or a spa treatment. But if you get bored—' he handed her a folder '—here's the full spec on the cocktail party. Everything else you have. Call me if you need anything. Otherwise I'll see you in the morning.'

A moment later Catherine was in a buggy, being driven

along a narrow path to her cabin, hearing Darcy call out to Max that she'd be at his cabin to discuss various contracts once he'd settled in.

Meat cleaver, axe, ice pick. And a *chainsaw*!

Clearly Catherine herself was *de trop*. Not needed for the contracts discussion. Not really needed for the cocktail function—but she could check the file if she got *bored*, not because it was her *job* or anything! Not needed as a dinner companion...

Max had kissed her as if he'd suck the tastebuds right out of her less than forty-eight hours earlier—but now she got a metaphorical pat on the head, as if she was the neighbour's pet dog, while he holed up with a lilac-wearing blonde? If Max wasn't careful he'd be joining Darcy on the bathroom floor in her head, chainsawed in half.

The buggy came to an abrupt stop in what appeared to be a small clearing in the middle of the rainforest, jolting Catherine out of her murderous thoughts. She was disorientated for a moment, but then she saw the wooden stilts amongst the foliage and looked up. A tree-house? Her cabin was a *tree-house*!

She hurried up the steps and entered the most amazing room she'd ever stayed in. Honey-red polished wood floor, stark white walls, high ceilings, a massive four-poster bed hung with gauzy white curtains. Wooden beams and shutters. A deck with a wooden table and two chairs.

She walked out onto the deck to take in the view and found that the cabin was perched above a river. It was private and peaceful and perfect, and it made her wonder what the finished product at Kurrangii would look like.

She wished she could discuss it with Max right away, instead of being forced to *'look around, relax, have a swim or a spa treatment'* while he unzipped Darcy's lilac dress!

She'd always found rivers soothing, so she concentrated on the water, trying to calm down as she pondered what she was going to do about the unforseen blonde obstacle.

Deep breathing. *Calm, calm, calm...*

Knock, knock, knock.

Max?

Okay, not calm.

She hurried to open the door, only to find one of the resort staff standing there, holding out a can of shaving cream.

'Compliments of Ms Appleby,' he said.

Catherine took the can. Closed the door. Looked at the shaving cream.

And then she swept into the bathroom and liberated its contents down the toilet. 'Take that, *Maxie-T*,' she said, and flushed. 'Take *that*!'

By the time Darcy left Max's cabin she'd propositioned him three times and suggested he join her for dinner at a 'fab new place' in Port Douglas. He'd knocked her back, and back, and back, while trying to understand what the hell his recalcitrant libido was up to—because apparently it couldn't accept an offer of sex unless it came wearing a wool skirt, thick tights and a cardigan.

Catherine North.

So hot. And cold. And hot.

He'd started salivating the moment he saw her on the plane and hadn't stopped. He'd had to tell her to take the day off just to give himself a respite. And then he'd gone and read that scene she'd given him, searching fruitlessly for a reference to Alex's eye colour—*earth to Max, get over it!*—and now he wasn't only salivating, he was gagging for her. Because he knew a promise of sex when he read one, regardless of Alex's eye colour.

*How Jennifer wanted to touch him. His face, his hair. She wanted to grab his backside and pull him harder against her, where she was melting. But the rush of lust was too overpowering. First she had to wait, had to bend and take and feel. But she would have her turn. Soon she would touch and kiss. And it would be more than he'd ever dreamed of...*

Hello, permanent erection! Did Catherine really think that needed critiquing? She could critique it herself with one look at the front of his pants.

Max ran his hands tiredly through his hair and walked out onto the deck to try and clear his head—it was either that or re-read the scene he shouldn't have read in the first place, and those pages were already showing signs of over-handling. Disintegration by morning was a real possibility.

*Calm, calm, calm...* That was what he needed. Calm.

This resort had a magical setting. Everywhere you turned there was rainforest, dense and lush and green. Around every building and along every path bushes and trees clustered, as though promising to consume everything man-made.

He wondered what Catherine's reaction had been. She was perceptive, and always had something intelligent to say, and he'd found himself relying on her judgement more and more the longer they worked together. He wanted to know if she liked this setting. What she thought of the cabins. If she believed the Moss Falls' pool design—lagoon-style, with a waterfall at one end—would work at Kurrangii.

*Then you shouldn't have given her the day off, moron! Now, stop thinking about her.*

Tomorrow was time enough to hear her views.

Tomorrow.

When he would *not* brush against her as they passed each other in the meeting room, would *not* finger-graze her when he handed her a document, would *not* nudge her knee under the table.

Okay—he was petrified about tomorrow. Because if he had to specifically instruct himself not to do those things, he needed a libido adjustment. And okay, he already *knew* he needed that, from his reactions today.

He'd never found the prospect of plane sex remotely appealing, so how come seeing three undone shirt buttons had him instantly imagining crowding Cathy into the aircraft toilet, ripping off her underwear and shoving himself right into her?

And what was so wonderful about lemon perfume that it should be able to hammer-whack him in the head? Because that's what the smell of her had done to him when he'd leaned towards her in the car. He'd wanted to wrench her out of the seat and into the back, lay her down on the leather, dive under her hideous skirt and see how far down she dabbed it.

At least imagining the look on Darcy's face had he acted on that fantasy gave him a laugh.

Darcy clearly hadn't thought much of Catherine. And vice versa.

Darcy—his decoy. He'd figured that if Catherine thought he and Darcy were going at it she'd feel safer. And Catherine already seemed to have got the message, so he was glad he'd asked Darcy to come to the airport to get it established straight off the bat. Even if he had to put up with that ridiculous nickname.

He went back inside. Read the scene again. Cursed.

Okay—he might have given Catherine the day off, and she might have thought he was busy with Darcy...but she could have called him, couldn't she? She *had* to know he'd be interested in her views of this resort.

Or what about a quick call to...to ask if he had any work for her? To check if he wanted to go over tomorrow's agenda? To see if he needed...well...*anything*. Like...like dinner, for example!

Not that dinner was part of her job. Of course it wasn't.

But he was hungry, dammit!

And he should not be lurking in his cabin on the off-chance that Catherine would call and ask if he wanted to grab a bite and go over...something or other.

He should just go and eat!

*Without* Catherine North.

Because it was definitely not a good idea to eat dinner with a woman whose body you wanted to eat dinner *off.*

Okay—enough! Moss Falls had a great open-air bar and restaurant overlooking the pool. He would go there, grab a drink, eat something, then take a walk to stretch his legs and get his head together.

Max suppressed a sigh as he saw Darcy the instant he entered the bar. So much for her 'fab new place' in Port Douglas! She beckoned him over.

'What'll it be, Maxie-T?'

Looked as if he had a dinner companion. But mouth-to-skin food consumption was now officially off the menu.

Max was halfway through his chargrilled trout when he saw Catherine. Being led to a table on the restaurant balcony. Smiling as a waiter seated her.

Not wearing her glasses.

What did that mean? Did she not need them unless she was working with documents?

*What the hell does it matter?* his frazzled brain asked.

*It doesn't,* his sane self answered.

But somehow it *did*. Because she looked…different. Her hair wasn't down, but it wasn't in a bun either. It was in a ponytail, high on her crown, and the style made her eyes stand out and sharpened her cheekbones.

'Maxie-T, you've had your fork halfway to your mouth for a full thirty seconds. What's up?'

Max dragged his attention back to Darcy. 'Nothing,' he said.

But Darcy was already turning, seeing Catherine. 'Oh, it's your poor little assistant…all alone. Shall we ask her to join us?'

Without waiting for an answer, Darcy was up and off.

Throughout Max's professional association with Darcy he'd seen her sharpen her teeth and rip whole chunks out of 'rival' females. But there she was, sitting opposite Catherine, gesturing to Max. It was a safe bet she had no idea what was going through Max's X-rated mind when he looked at Catherine. Darcy probably imagined she would be shown to advantage next to the 'poor little assistant'.

The 'poor little assistant' didn't even spare him a glance.

She spoke to Darcy, her eyes narrowed, her lips pinched, and she shook her head—emphatic.

It seemed Catherine wouldn't be joining them.

Huh.

Darcy came gliding back over. 'She says we seem to be well advanced so she'll leave us to it. Which makes sense.'

'Yes. Perfect sense,' Max agreed, and heard the curtness that meant he was hanging on to his patience by a thread. He took a bite of fish, tasted *nothing*, laid down his cutlery. 'I'm done,' he said. Same curt voice. He needed to see Catherine. Alone. Right now. He didn't have time to eat chargrilled fish!

Darcy pouted. 'No dessert?'

'Not for me.'

Foot tapping, Max waited for Darcy to finish her spaghetti whatever-the-hell-it-was, then order a caramel tart that took an age to be delivered as he kept an inconspicuous eye on Catherine's table. At least he hoped it was an inconspicuous eye and not a swooping eagle eye—but he couldn't swear to it. He could feel each breath he took as he watched, because he counted through them, controlling them.

Catherine's plate had been cleared, and she was slanting a long look out at the night, all dreamy-eyed. Thinking... *what*? He would love to know. Then she was reaching for her phone. Smiling at the screen. Text message? Yes, because she seemed to be texting back. Long message. *Loooong*. Still going.

Who the hell was she texting?

Next thing, she was calling for her bill. She was signing. Picking up the purse she'd laid on the table. Looking inside. Retrieving her cabin key. She was leaving—and Darcy was only halfway through her caramel tart. Right. *He wanted to leave*. Now. Leave. *Now!*

He had to know where Catherine was going and who she'd been texting and if she was meeting someone.

None of which was any of his business.

Catherine looked over at him. No smile, but she sent a small wave his way—very hello-boss-from-uninterested-employee—as she left the table. She walked to the restaurant entrance, spoke to the *maître-d'*...

Then Darcy said something, so Max had to redirect his attention to her, and when he checked the entrance again Catherine was gone.

Goddammit!

'Darcy,' he said, interrupting he knew not what, 'I need to speak to Catherine—a problem about the morning. Sorry, but I'm going to have to leave you.'

Darcy acquiesced, albeit with a pout. Followed by the offer of an in-cabin nightcap—hastily declined.

And then Max was off.

Chasing after Catherine. Who probably did not want to be chased.

But enough was enough.

# CHAPTER EIGHT

MAX KNEW WHICH cabin Catherine was in so he headed in that direction, and saw her—*yes*!—a metre shy of it. She was walking slowly and had that dreamy look again. The way she looked when she was gazing out of his office window. Thinking about a scene for *Passion Flower*, maybe...?

Like...Alex calling out to Jennifer to wait for him... Walking to her... Taking hold of her... Backing her against a handy tree trunk... Moving his thigh between hers as he raised her skirt, fingers moving up, between her thighs, into her wet heat... The sounds of the rainforest alive around them as his fingers slid inside...

Holy Mother of God, he wanted to do that to Catherine.

'Cathy!' he called out.

She turned, her fingers jumping to where the top button of her shirt was done up. And his brain snapped back. She did that when she was stressed. He was stressing her—and that was *before* he backed her against a handy tree trunk and shoved his thigh between her legs.

Her fingers dropped. 'Do you need something?' she asked, all businesslike, walking back to him.

'I just... I just...' *Have no idea what I'm doing!* 'Yes. Yes, I do.'

*Think fast, think fast.*

The heat settled around them. The silence. Except it wasn't dead silence. It was alive. Water trickling, frogs, leaves rustling. Some weird insect noise. A plop-plop in the river. He could smell that lemon fragrance of hers. Stronger in the heat. He wanted to lick it off her.

'Well?' she asked.

'We should go over tomorrow's agenda.'

'Now?'

'Why not now?'

There was a challenge in that which he hadn't intended. It reminded him of the way he'd put the Queensland trip to her—playing the boss card, almost *daring* her to say no. Just because he'd got all hot and achy and…and hot…in the filing alcove and it had freaked him out that she could do that to him. Like he was freaked out now, chasing her when he'd been determined not to.

'Unless you're meeting someone?'

*Damn.* That had come out all belligerent too. Clearly he needed to look up the words 'sledgehammer' and 'subtle' in the dictionary and learn the difference.

'No, I'm not meeting anyone. Now is fine. Where?'

Stab of relief. Out of all proportion.

'My cabin.'

Hmm, that sounded like another challenge. He had to stop that. 'It's got a separate area I use for meetings, in case you're wondering.'

Okay, *that* was just pathetic.

'Why would I be wondering?' she asked, sounding amused. 'I do *occasionally* book your accommodation.'

'I just meant— I mean, we can go somewhere else, somewhere more public, if you'd feel more comfortable. After Friday night.'

And so much for not having to talk about Friday night ever again!

'After Friday night?' she repeated slowly. And then she stepped closer. 'Are you saying if we're alone together you're going to kiss me, Max?'

'Huh?' Clearly an intelligent response was beyond him. Probably because he *did* want to kiss her. Right then. Right there.

*Earth to Max...earth to Max...get a grip! Not going to so much as* breathe *on her, remember?*

Catherine gave him what could only be termed a superior smile, and stepped back again. 'No need to have a conniption, Max. Remember how you wanted me to tell you when you were being stupid? I'm just calling it, that's all. Because I know it's acceptable to work from your cabin.'

'Good. Because it is. Acceptable. And...and safe. For you, I mean.' Oh, he was stupid, all right. *And* pathetic.

'Do I need my computer?'

'No, but what about your glasses? Don't you need them?'

'No, I do not,' she said shortly, and gave him the death stare.

*Okaaaay.* Glasses were not a subject for discussion, then.

Wow, this was going to be fun! Him tense. Her bristling like a cactus. No buffer between them. And forbidden lust clawing at him like a wild thing. *Forbidden lust?* He'd be writing his own romance novel soon.

They walked in uncomfortable silence to his cabin—which was more like a house, set amongst the foliage and edging the river. Catherine's eyes widened as she took in the expansive living space, the wide glass doors opening onto a huge deck.

'Can I get you something?' he asked. 'A drink? Coffee?'

'I'm fine.' She walked around the room. 'Is Darcy joining us?'

'No. Why would she be?'

'From the way things seemed in the car, and the fact she was with you this afternoon, I thought maybe you needed her involved in *everything*.' A raised eyebrow. Very cool. 'Unless that wasn't work? This afternoon, I mean?'

He took a step towards her. 'There's nothing going on between me and Darcy.' *Okaaay*, so much for using Darcy as a decoy.

Catherine's lips pinched in. 'Isn't there? She's blonde. Tall. *Horsey.* Your usual type.'

Blonde, tall—okay. But horsey? He couldn't help

himself—he laughed. 'And when did you last see one of these...these fillies...prancing around on my arm?'

'Two and a half months ago. Leah. She was the third in just my first month at Rutherford Property. Impressive.'

'So where have all these tall blondes been since Leah?' he asked. 'And why am I stuck here with a short brunette?'

'Not so stuck you didn't arrange to have a tall blonde waiting for you.' She took a step closer. 'And frankly, Max, you could do better.'

She gave that head-toss Max had never seen her do until today in the car—and he had to say it worked better with a swinging ponytail than it had with a bun.

'You're giving me *dating* advice?' he asked, laughing again. God, she was just...*brilliant*. 'Okay, let me have it. What's wrong with Darcy?'

'Other than the fact she's condescending?'

Before he could respond—and God knew what he would have said to that, anyway—she jabbed him in the chest with an irate finger.

'Do you know what she said to me?'

No, he didn't, but he was suddenly dying to hear it.

Head-toss. 'She *said*, "I see you've done the sensible thing and abandoned your specs. Good for you." *Good for you?* How utterly— How—' But words seemed to fail her. She made an explosive sound of frustration. And then, suddenly finding the word, she flung it at him: *'Outrageous.'*

Max could feel his lip twitch and ruthlessly subdued it. But, God, he was enjoying this. Like the volcanic eruptions she sometimes treated him to in the office, only magnified— *superb*.

'So you're sensitive about your glasses. How was she to know?'

'I am *not* sensitive about my glasses. I am myopic. I wear glasses. Full-stop.'

'You nearly snapped my head off a few minutes ago when I asked you about them.'

'That was a hangover effect. From *her*. I wear contact lenses sometimes! So what?'

'Yes—so what?' Max agreed mildly, and saw her temper surge again. 'Why did it bother you?'

'It just— I just— Oh, never mind...*Maxie-T.*'

'The T is for Thomas, if you're interested, *South.*'

'The South is for North, if you're interested—but I'm *not*. Interested.'

'Yes, you are, or you wouldn't have mentioned it.'

'She's condescending.'

'And Rick's a tattooed freak. So what?'

'Tattoooed—?' She broke off. He could practially *see* her teeth grinding with rage.

'Just don't send her over to ask me to join you for dinner again.'

'I didn't send her.'

Catherine's eyes locked on to him. Sizzling. He wondered if the top of her head was about to be blown off. *Wow!* And then, with a visible effort, she reined everything back in.

'I see.'

'You see what, Cathy?' Max asked, and found he was holding his breath for the answer.

'That everything really *is* ruined. There's no going back.'

'Nothing is ruined, and we *are* going back,' he said. Holding his breath again. What did he want her to say to that? *What?*

She glared at him. 'Then why didn't you need me today?'

'Why didn't you call to *ask* if I needed you?'

Hair toss. Girly and gorgeous. 'You're the boss. You call, I come running—it doesn't happen in reverse.'

'It's never been like that with us and you know it.'

'We didn't even go over tomorrow's agenda.'

'We're doing that now.'

'Are you *trying* to be obtuse?'

Max's hands went for his head. He dragged in a long, deep breath and released it suddenly.

'Ah, hell—all right. I should have had you at the meeting with Darcy. We should have looked at the agenda earlier. We should have discussed the week ahead over dinner. But I didn't call you and I didn't involve you because I didn't want to put you in an uncomfortable situation so soon after Friday night.'

'I'm not scared of you, Max. I *trust* you. Get it? And, for the record, I have a punishing right knee and I know how to use it—*if* I want to.'

She looked up at him and he could see it...trust.

She trusted him. God, that made his chest hurt.

They were so close he could see the tiny green and gold flecks in her eyes amongst the brown. *Beautiful.* He could see the rapid rise and fall of her chest as her breaths came in short bursts. How could she trust him when all he could think about when he looked at her was kissing her again?

'But I don't want to use it,' she said, and her voice had gone all husky. 'So go right ahead and kiss me whenever you want. Like...say...now...'

Had she just read his mind?

'Cathy, you *do* realise I'm trying to do the right thing, don't you? And that's not my default setting so you *could* meet me halfway.'

'I'm not meeting you anywhere while you're tiptoeing around me. I'm going to go mad if you keep that up.'

'And I'm going to go mad if you don't back off.'

'Well, I'm not backing off, so get ready for your strait-jacket.'

'Cathy, you can't really want another boss touching you.'

'Well, I do. So if you have a problem with that you're going to have to sack me.' She sounded dismissive—but she'd reached for her earring, twirling it nervously.

'Sack you...?' Max felt that ache in his chest again. 'Okay, I think I get the whole sacking obsession. It's what he did, isn't it? Threatened to sack you because you wouldn't do what he wanted. And now you keep daring *me* to do it. Just to test my mettle. That's trust, is it?'

He saw the little jolt of reaction. The sudden vulnerability. Max didn't make a habit of hugging his assistants, but he wanted to hug *her*. Just until she got her fire back. That was all.

'So you're not going to sack me even if I hit on you?' she asked, dogged.

'This is crazy. You're not hitting on me and I'm not sacking you.'

'Yes, Max, I *am* hitting on you. I'm hitting on you now.' Step closer. 'Did you read it? The scene I gave you?'

*Damn.* The words were there, in his head, almost memorised. He nodded. Swallowed.

'That's me hitting on you.'

'I'm not the one for you.'

'Why not?'

'Because I'm your boss.'

'It didn't stop you on Friday night.'

'Yes, Cathy, it did.'

'Oh, I see... It stopped you. When I told you...'

She frowned, looking so uncertain he wanted to hug her again.

And then she said slowly, 'But if I hadn't told you...?' She gave him a tiny glimmering smile. 'We would have kissed again, and ended up in bed. So it's not a case of you not being attracted to me.'

*Whoa.* He had to head this off. Why, why, *why* had he chased her?

*You know why. You* know.

'The thing is,' he said, ignoring that unhelpful voice in his head, 'I've got form...history...when it comes to people like RJ. No—don't interrupt! Just hear me out. Because I don't talk about this and it's not...easy.' Pause. 'My father has been hitting on his secretaries since... Well, who really knows when? He certainly didn't wait long before moving his secretary into the house after my mother died. A month, that's all—so you'd have to say it wasn't a brand-new relationship, right?'

'Oh, Max.'

'Janelle, her name was. She arrived the day before my thirteenth birthday. She even baked me a cake. She didn't last, of course. Neither did the next one, Tracy. Or Kelly. Patricia. Elaine. Or any of the many, many others. Flip—that's my father's name, which is appropriate given the way he flips women—moved some of them into the house and kept others on the side. But they all had one thing in common—thinking Flip meant it when he told them it would last forever. Which I guess is what he promised my mother. At least she got a *version* of forever, I guess.'

Catherine had gone all doe-eyed as she looked at him and Max felt his heart lurch. The way it had lurched all those years ago for his mother, when he'd wondered if she'd *known* what a bastard her husband was. The way it had lurched on Friday night for Catherine, who definitely knew how vile men could be.

'I'm sorry about your mother,' Catherine said gently. 'How did she die?'

'Car accident.'

'And do you think—? Did she…know? About Janelle?'

Max rubbed his hands over his face. 'That's not relevant.'

'Of course it is,' she said, and touched his hand—the first time she'd ever laid a voluntary finger on him.

It was so brief he shouldn't have even felt it…and yet he did. Everywhere.

'So much to take at any age—let alone at thirteen,' she said.

'I hope she didn't know, but she probably did,' he found himself answering, because somehow that instant of connection had made him want to tell her. Because it *was* relevant. Max's whole modus operandi with women stemmed from it.

'And it was hard—seeing your father with those women, *hating* him, when you were grieving and you needed him.' It was a statement, not a question.

He couldn't trust himself to speak because his heart was lurching again. Because Catherine just *knew*. And he wished, wished, *wished* he could hold on to her.

'And that's not me getting all "psychological",' she said. Another small, warm touch on his hand. 'I've seen the photos on your desk—that's how I know. You with your mother. The bond, the love. But no father-son photos.'

Max looked down at his hand. His fingers were flexing where she'd touched him, as if he could still feel it. 'The thing is, Cathy—and this brings us to our situation—my father always blames the girls.'

She nodded. 'Like RJ.'

'Exactly. *They* come on to *him*. Put out lures, entice him, dress to attract him. And then, when it's over, they have to get out of the office, too—and there's another creative list of excuses. Their shoddy work. Their unprofessionalism. Even a lack of morality once—what a joke!'

'I understand all that. But from what I know of you, you don't promise anyone forever, like he does. Am I right?'

'Right. But—'

'No buts. And you don't need a lame excuse to get your assistants into bed, right?'

'Until you, no.'

'Me? But I'm no different from the others.'

He laughed. 'Oh, my God, you are. The way you look, the way you act, the way you work. There was no chink in your armour, so I used *Passion Flower* as my excuse.'

'Well, I'm glad *something* good came out of that book,' she said, and he found himself speechless. 'But I don't accept it was some lame excuse,' she continued, 'and you didn't get me into bed, anyway.'

'No, because you didn't—'

'Don't say it! You could have—and you didn't. So stop pretending to be a monster when you're not. You might cut a swathe through your own personal assistants, but that in itself doesn't turn you into your father. You're not unscrupulous enough to be him.'

'A *swathe*?' Max was revolted. 'I don't cut *swathes*. It's not like I'm fishing in one pool of captive fish at a trout farm.'

'Well, they all seem to be the same tall, blonde, horse-faced species. But I'll grant you that you fish in a few ponds—models, lawyers, doctors, teachers, the typing pool...'

'*Typing* pool? You're not a damned typist, Cathy.'

'Oh—so you *are* fishing in my pool?'

'I'm not— That's not— Look, you're different. You're already too free and easy with the resignations and I'm not risking you.'

'But all those other assistants were riskable?'

'Stop with the "all those". It was only ever a couple. Three, maybe. All right—four. But no more than that—and knowing now how close I've sailed to Flip territory, I won't do it again. But the answer to your question is that they should not have been *"riskable"* either. But at least they were all more experienced than you. They all knew the score.'

'If they all knew the score, how come they ended up leaving?'

'Because they— They— They wanted more.'

'Sounds to me like they *didn't* know the score. Sex not love—right, Max? Well, I'm fine with that. I *want* that. *Love* would have me packing up my desk. Now. I've given you the RJ story. You've told me about your father. We both know the score. So let's go.'

'You don't know the *score*. And it's not just about whether someone ends up wanting more, either. It's about— It's— Look, you're a baby when it comes to this stuff. I can tell from *Passion Flower*.'

Her eyes narrowed. 'What about *Passion Flower*?' she asked, and there was a warning in it.

He pushed it with a laugh. 'I've done a lot—a *lot*—more than Alex Taylor. So much more it would scare poor little Jennifer Andrews out of her wits.'

'You're saying Alex needs character development?'

Another laugh. 'His character's not the issue. His character's nice and romantic—which gives the lie to your sex-not-love mantra. But sexually...?' He shook his head. 'Nope.

And the reason he doesn't have the moves is because the writer isn't ready for them.'

'If you're so hot you can teach me. Show me.'

Okay—tactical error. 'I don't *do* sweet little virgins.'

Her temper was glowing nicely, but she stepped closer. 'If I really stood there in your arms like a block of wood on Friday night then I need help. Because that wasn't how I was feeling. If I'm scared to touch it's because of what RJ Harrow did to me. And I don't want him to be the yardstick by which I measure every sexual relationship I have for the rest of my life. A friend would help me.'

'I'm not your friend, I'm your boss. Find another guy.'

'But you're the guy I trust.'

'Well, you shouldn't trust me,' he said, short and sharp. 'Because I don't trust myself.' Sigh. Deep and tired. 'Let me spell this out: I am not nice. I'll never love a woman the way Alex loves Jennifer.'

'Why not?'

'Because I won't do to a woman what was done to my mother. I'd have to be so sure—so very, *very* sure—that a woman would be the *last* woman before I let it happen. And you know what? You can never be sure. Which means it will never happen.'

'And that's why you never keep an assistant for long? They always fall in love with you?'

'Bingo.'

'Now, you see—that's *nice!*' Catherine said.

'*What?*'

'Warning me. It's unnecessary—but sweet of you.' Head-toss. 'Let me spell this out: I am not nice either. And I won't love you.'

'People have said that before—and fallen. And with you...' Sigh. 'I don't want to hurt you, Cathy.'

'You won't. You *can't*. Not more than—' She broke off. 'You won't.'

She turned her back on him and he came up behind her, hands hovering uselessly near her shoulders. He wanted so badly to touch her. Hair, collar—he'd take *anything*. But touching her was what had got them into this mess.

He stuck his hands under his armpits, out of harm's way. Then, annoyed at his lack of control, unstuck them.

'The thing is, Cathy, what happens if I touch you, and you freak out?'

'You'll stop.'

'Will I? Even I don't know that. What if I don't? What if I push on, say it was your fault for tempting me? What happens then?'

She spun to face him, but he put a finger on her lips.

'Shh. That's rhetorical. Because I know the answer. You'll run for the exit, flinging your resignation at me. And that's not happening, got it? Not. Happening. So, Cathy, go right ahead and goad me, taunt me and tempt me, undo your buttons, wear your contact lenses, change your hairstyle. Whatever you do, I won't touch you again.'

Catherine's hands went to her buttons. 'Well, let's test that.'

'*What* are you doing?'

'You told me to undo my buttons.'

He stared at her as everything in him urged him touch her again. To kiss her. To be so damned good this time she would *have* to respond. And that would mean...*what*? When that happened he could...could... He had no idea what he could do. So he just stood there, indecisive in a way he'd never been in his life.

But then her fingers moved up to her ear to twist the little gold hoop and Max released the breath he'd been holding in one forceful huff.

'See where your fingers are?'

Her hand dropped immediately, went back to her buttons.

'Too late. Trust me, Cathy—you're not ready.'

She strode over to the French doors, stared out at the blackness. Her right hand fisted as if she was going to punch through the glass. She stamped her foot. Once. Twice.

'I wish I'd never told you.'

He could see her reflected in the glass. See her bra through the gaping front of her shirt. His hands went to his hair again, yanked it. She was going to make him bald!

'Well, you *did* tell me, Cathy,' he said, and his voice was sharper than he'd intended because she was making it so painful. He *wanted* her—clenched fists, stamping foot, flashing eyes, starched shirt, wool skirt...everything. 'And this is where we are. With me horny as hell and you giving me grief.'

She turned. 'You know, Max, a boss isn't supposed to tell his employee he's horny. I'm pretty sure that's sexual harassment. Maybe I *will* haul you up on charges—if you don't get over here and *kiss me*!'

Max had a sudden blinding understanding. *She* was the passion flower. Unfurling. The head-tossing, the foot-stamping, the unleashed temper—each of them was a petal. She'd never done any of that before. Until he'd kissed her.

Undoing her buttons on the plane?

Demanding that he kiss her?

Prim and proper *Cathy*?

She was hunting him. And he *loved* it!

'Max,' she said, so huffy he wanted to lick her, 'you're not being fair. Because I'm horny as hell too. And I don't have a Darcy stashed somewhere.'

He stepped closer. 'Neither do I!' he said. 'I haven't had a Darcy stashed for two and a half months, thanks to you.'

'Thanks to me?' She smiled. Feline. Gorgeous. 'I think that means you want to have sex with me, Max.'

*Horny.* She was horny, too.

Well, he'd tried, hadn't he? But he'd always known he wasn't a saint!

'Right,' he said. 'One kiss. Let's see what happens.'

'Make it a good one,' she ordered.

# CHAPTER NINE

'FOR THE RECORD, Catherine North, I don't know how to make it bad,' Max said—and pulled her in so quickly she stumbled.

Or at least she would have stumbled if he hadn't snatched her off her feet and plastered her against him.

And it was more than a kiss. Because as his mouth swooped, as he forced his tongue inside before she even had a chance to part her lips, he grabbed her backside and lifted her higher, mashing her right onto his pelvis.

She was so shocked she couldn't move. But it was *wonderful*. She was instantly aroused. Aching with it. Horny didn't begin to cover it. Delirious came closer. Delirious with need.

Max's was mouth on hers, his heart thudding against hers, his breaths tangling with hers. He was rubbing himself against her as though he would plunge into her through the thick, confining skirt. *Damned skirt*. Keeping her legs trapped when they really wanted to curl themselves around him. She wished he would tumble her onto the couch, the floor—*anywhere*—and rip her clothes off.

Instead Max stood there, holding her off the floor, kissing her so hard she was sure her lips would be bruised. And then he suddenly released her, dropping her back onto her feet.

He kept his eyes on her as she swallowed, as one of her hands instinctively reached for her top button, felt skin, then gripped the gaping edges, clutching them together.

She saw the look in Max's eyes, the shift from passion to

weariness as he took in her fingers gripping her shirt, and she cursed silently in her head.

'Just what a man wants to see—a woman buttoning up after he kisses her,' he said. 'And *that's* why I don't do virgins.'

She forced her hands to drop. 'I'm not a virgin.'

'Maybe not technically.' He ran a hand into his hair as he sighed. 'Cathy, I'm offering you the chance—*one* chance—to put a stop to this insanity. Stop poking the bear if you're not sure you can handle the response.'

'I can handle anything you dish out.'

'You didn't handle that kiss so well. And that's not even the best one in my arsenal.'

She stared at him. *Blink, blink, blink.* Trembling lip. 'You really *don't* want me?'

'Just the fact that you can even *ask* that tells me—'

She watched the emotions chase across his face. Lust. Tenderness. Incredulity. Frustration. And then—*bingo.* He smiled grimly.

'Going all girly on me, Cathy? Well, save it. You know I want you. And, yes, I know I can have you, too. *If* I want to feel like a depraved monster—taking someone who isn't up to my weight. Oddly enough, I'm not too crazy about feeling like a depraved monster—and all that button-grabbing is going to get very old, very fast. So save the blinky, trembly-lip stuff and *think.* Carefully.'

'I can take your weight!' she insisted, although her limbs and her voice were shaking.

'*Can* you? Be sure. Because I'm not a toy or a lapdog. Or even particularly civilised—especially not in bed. If you think you're getting Sir Galahad, think again.'

She threw back her shoulders. 'I don't want Sir Galahad.'

'Just as well—because he has now officially left the building and is working in a burger joint with Elvis somewhere.'

He did that stare—right through her pupils. And then he nodded. 'All right, consider the line irrevocably crossed, little passion flower. I'll help you unfurl your petals. But it's going to be done to *my* timetable, and on *my* terms, and until I say you're ready, you're not. So…you wait. Got it?'

'How will I know when the time is right?'

Low, sexy laugh. 'You'll know. It will be when you're so hot you'll think you've got lava in your bloodstream.'

For one moment he looked at her, and then—shocking her even more than the kiss had—he pulled her in, hugged her, ran his hand over her ponytail. He pulled back, looked down at her. Smiled that slow, lopsided smile and turned her knees to jelly.

'So, now can we do the agenda?'

And Catherine, who suddenly wasn't quite so sure of herself after all, could only nod.

Catherine took exquisite care with her appearance the next morning. Just a little change—enough to start the ball rolling. The glasses were back on, her hair was in its usual tight chignon, she was wearing a businesslike brown skirt and her shoes were nana-heeled brown pumps. *But* her legs were bare and her top was fluttery daffodil-yellow silk.

She was the first in the room at the resort's conference facility, double-checking the arrangements. She adjusted name cards, ensured everyone was positioned at the table appropriate to their level of participation—with herself next to Max, set out folders of materials at each spot, tested the audio-visual equipment, and organised for beverages and snacks to be available throughout the day.

Max came in fifteen minutes after Catherine, full of energy. He stopped as he took in what she was wearing and said, 'Huh…' Or at least his mouth made the shape of it but no actual sound emerged. And Catherine felt a curl low in her belly as his face went taut and dark.

If she could achieve that just with a yellow top and knee-to-ankle flesh, she couldn't wait to see how he coped as the week wore on and she progressively deconstructed herself.

That night, for the first business dinner, Catherine wore the glasses and the chignon, but changed into a cotton trouser suit teamed with a skimpy camisole—and had the satisfaction of seeing Max's jaw actually drop.

The next morning: glasses, businesslike but expertly tailored skirt, hot pink short-sleeved top, and the chignon replaced with a messy bun on top of her head.

Max's teeth were clamped so tightly as he took in the differences she thought she'd be hunting down paracetamol before the day was too advanced.

That night's dinner—an even looser bun and a form-fitting wrap dress in mint-green that displayed a generous hint of cleavage.

She saw Max take a deep breath and walked over to him, smiling. 'Everything okay?' she asked sweetly.

'No.'

'What's wrong?'

Max's jaw worked for a moment, but nothing emerged.

'Well, if nothing's wrong, I'd better get back to it,' Catherine said.

'Back to what?'

'Making sure everything's on track.'

'It's on track.'

'So why are you looking like that?'

'Like what?'

'Morose.'

'Because—' Cut off. Another breath. Tiny shake of the head. One more breath. 'Why aren't you sitting with the guests? This is the second night in a row.'

Hmm, that clearly was *not* the real 'because'…but one hairpin at a time. 'I prefer to float and make sure everything goes smoothly. I had something to eat in my room, so I'm fed and watered.'

'Which would be fine if you were a horse,' he snapped.

'You would know, as an equine aficionado. All those coltish blondes…'

'Well, Cathy, thanks to our little deal, the only coltish blond I'm touching on this trip is our PR guy, Doug. Are you coming to dinner with the two of us tomorrow night?'

'Actually, I have a…a sort of date tomorrow night.'

One long, hot stare. Then Max scanned the restaurant. 'Which one?'

'None of these guys.'

'You haven't had time to meet anyone else.'

'It's someone I've known forever. He lives up here.'

Tight, tight smile. 'Good for you. But, just so you know, once you touch another man I'm out of the game.'

'Then tonight, at least, you're still *in* the game—aren't you?'

Another long, hot look. 'You're right. And I'm playing the boss card. Take a seat. You're joining us for dinner.'

'I thought—'

'Boss card, Catherine. Sit the hell down.'

The boss card. *Ugh.* Max seemed to play that particular card whenever he was reminding her of the boss/employee dynamic. Almost as if he was pushing her away. Which was *not* what she'd had in mind for tonight.

Sighing, Catherine adjusted the place cards at one of the tables, positioning herself between one of Rutherford Property's junior engineers and a young marketing manager. They were the best-looking men in the room—aside from Max— and, given the set of Max's mouth when he'd made that remark about her touching another man, she had a feeling her choice of seat would irk him. Which served him right for playing the boss card.

She was so girly and charming over dinner she was making herself sick—but the increasingly surly looks Max was flinging at her across the room made it worthwhile. And then she laughed—too loudly—and Max actually glared at her.

Right. Time for another little push!

One of Catherine's responsibilities was to ensure that Max circulated. It was relatively easy to steer him towards people at cocktail functions, where people were always moving. Dinners were trickier, because she had to watch for briefly vacated seats that Max could occupy for a quick hello. If Catherine had been floating she would have been able to walk into Max's line of sight and give him a subtle head or hand gesture. But tonight, *not* floating, by order of the boss, called for something a little more definite.

She watched the tables and the instant a seat opened up—at the table next to hers—excused herself and headed for Max. She put her hand on his shoulder, letting a finger slip subtly above his shirt collar to touch his neck. Just the tiniest touch. It might almost have been an accident.

But Max shivered.

And, *oooohhh*, she felt it. The power...

Before the shiver had worked itself through his body she leaned down close to his ear, cupping a hand to cover her mouth as though whispering something confidential. 'Table Three...' she said—very *Happy Birthday, Mr President.*

Max shivered again, and started to put down his wine glass, but Catherine wasn't finished. She leaned in as though for another whisper...and let the tip of her tongue touch behind his earlobe. One tiny, tiny lick.

Max's arm jerked and three drops of red wine spilled onto the white tablecloth before he could stabilise his glass. And then, with an abrupt, 'Excuse me,' he stood. With a darkling look at Catherine, who glided serenely back to her own table, he made his way to the empty seat.

Catherine knew she would have to produce something more definitive than a one-second lick if she was to get Max into bed by Friday, but at least it was a start.

She wasn't feeling quite so sanguine five minutes later, when a hand suddenly descended on her shoulder. She didn't have to look up to know it was Max—because she'd seen him leave Table Three and smelled him as he arrived behind her—but she still flinched.

'I hope Catherine's been looking after you?' he said genially to the table at large.

One of Max's potential investors smiled at the two of them. 'Very well!' he said. 'She's been advising me on residential property investment in her old stomping ground, Abu Najmah.'

'Has she? What did she say?'

Catherine glanced up at Max, caught the arrested look on his face, and decided 'she' could speak for herself. 'I said that although the market bottomed out a couple of years ago there are still bargains to be had because of a chronic over-supply.'

Max gave her shoulder a squeeze and his little finger touched the skin where her neck met her shoulder. Lingered there. And even knowing it was pure and simple payback, Catherine's mouth went dry.

Fortunately the investor took up the narrative. 'Catherine recommends buying at a maximum twenty-five per cent above estimated construction and reasonable land costs and watching that potential fancy finishes aren't included in the price. Within those parameters, she says rental yields of up-wards of four per cent are possible, which should limit the downside in any future debt crisis.'

'I think she's angling for my job,' Max said with a laugh, and she heard something in his voice that made her look up at him again.

He was smiling at her—a strange smile. Kind of... *proud*. Wondering... And for the briefest moment Catherine couldn't seem to help relaxing her head so that her cheek grazed his hand.

And then he was gone.

He didn't come near her for the rest of the night—didn't even look at her. And she didn't go near him either. Because things felt suddenly...complicated.

When she'd let herself into her cabin she headed straight for the deck so she could gaze at the river, remembering his scent, the texture of his skin, the taste of it, on the tip of her tongue, the feel of his hand on her shoulder, the smile on his mouth but also in his eyes.

When the knock on the door came her heart started that gallop she couldn't seem to conrol. She was blushing as she went to the door, so sure it was Max. That this was it. The time. Because of the way he'd looked at her...

But it was one of the resort staff, presenting an envelope. She took it, closed the door, then sagged with relief.

With…relief? *Oh, my God.* She was *relieved.* How twisted was *that*? She should be sagging with disappointment—not *relief.*

She slid onto the couch as the ramifications hit. *She wasn't ready.*

She stared blindly at the envelope in her hands. Took a few deep breaths. No, she wouldn't accept that. It was just… Just that smile. The way he'd smiled at her. That smile had not been a getting-you-into-bed-tonight smile. It had been a something-else smile. Something almost…frightening.

She didn't want to think about what the smile meant and why it had affected her so much. She just wanted to have sex with him. Why did that suddenly not feel simple?

She felt a shiver ripple through her—the way that shiver had run through Max when she'd put her tongue on his skin—and looked at the envelope, at her name scrawled in Max's bold handwriting. It made her shiver again.

She ripped open the envelope, removed the sheets of paper. It was probably another boss-card instruction. Well, he could take his boss card and—

*Ooooohhhh!* The shiver ripped through her again. And again.

*'I hope you like water,' Alex said to Jennifer as he waded into the private pool with her in his arms. 'Because I'm going to make you wet.'*

*He lowered her, manoeuvring her so that her legs wrapped around him as the water settled. Her arms were around his shoulders. His were around her hips. The look in his eyes, deep as sin, promised a fantasy.*

*But under the water he was hard against her sex— and that was the reality. Huge, throbbing, poised at her entrance. He dipped his head to take her mouth and she moaned…*

Lava. Hot. Wet. Racing through her.

All Catherine's uncertainty vanished.

If he thought he could send her that—stringing her along with a few new moves for Alex without fronting up in person…?

Well, game on.

The next morning—Wednesday, with only two days to go to the cocktail party—Catherine upped the ante. No glasses. Floaty beige dress cinched in at the waist. Nude sandals two inches higher than usual. Hair in a loose braid.

Darcy gave her a dagger-like stare—which she enjoyed immensely.

And Max, after a single sharp breath, turned his back on her.

Excellent.

She gave it a little push with a surreptitious knee-nudge under the table as the meeting got underway. Max's breath hung suspended for a split second—and then he edged away. When she did it a second time she got a glare. A third time and he reached under the table, gave her knee a retaliatory grab, and then edged his hand up, up, up, until she gasped. One last warning squeeze, right at the top of her thigh, and then the hand was gone.

Catherine desisted after that—because it was one thing trying to give a guy grief by making him horny as hell but quite another squirming around on your chair, trying to accommodate the achy throb between your legs as you pictured Alex Taylor lifting Jennifer Andrews out of her seat and jamming her on his lap in front of a roomful of serious-faced people.

Torture. Utter torture.

'Torture': word of the day.

The *whole* damned day.

Because whenever Max leaned closer to ask her to remind him of a key fact, or to jot down a special mention—so carefully *not* touching her again—she became an amorphous mass of raw arousal. She became Jennifer in the pool, legs wrapped around Alex. She became a hot scorch of flowing, surging, bubbling lava.

And there was nothing immediately do-able about it because *she* would be spending the evening with her brother and *Max* would be heading to Cairns with Doug. Which was probably just as well—because she wasn't certain a person couldn't die from an excess of unassuaged arousal, and Max wasn't doing much assuaging!

Once the meeting's participants had disappeared, Catherine packed up. Max had retreated to the end of the room with his phone stuck to his ear, so she gave him a series of I'm-out-of-here hand gestures—only to be furiously motioned to stay where she was. *Exactly* where she was.

Catherine could recognise the boss card, even in mime, so she stayed.

Into her head popped a memory of RJ on the phone in D.C., yelling at her about the seating plan just to trick her, and her throat tightened. Stupid—so stupid. Because Max wouldn't trick her. Max didn't have to. She would be perfectly happy for Max to shove her against the nearest wall and stick his tongue down her throat; he didn't need an excuse to get her alone and vulnerable.

But when Max came striding towards her she couldn't seem to help grabbing for her earring. Reflex.

'Okay—what the hell is going on?' he asked.

'Going on with...?'

'You.'

'I don't underst—'

'The clothes.'

She stared at him for a moment as that frisson of uncertainty faded. As she understood that this was *good*, not bad. Finally—*finally*—Max was acknowledging the change in her appearance in words, not scowls.

'You have a problem with my clothes?' she asked, throwing in an innocently confused blink.

'Knock off the girly stuff, Cathy. All the clothes were returned to Sandra—I checked. So where did that come from? And the green dress? The pink and yellow tops?'

Catherine tossed her head. 'Well, Max, when you were expressing your disdain for my appearance you didn't bother to *ask* if I had suitable clothing—either for this climate *or* this calibre of event.'

'Why would I think you had anything suitable? You haven't exhibited any sartorial flair in the office. And, going on what I've seen you wearing all damned summer, I had a real fear you'd drop dead from heat stroke on day one if I didn't step in. And I also thought— I thought—' His hands were digging in his hair.

'Thought...?'

'I thought you couldn't afford the clothes you'd need for here! All right?'

*Oh, my God, oh, my God.* He was embarrassed to be caught out caring. Again! Complication. Because that hit her right in the chest. Like an ache. She'd been so furious about the clothes...and all he'd wanted to do was save her from death and penury.

'Well, now you know I can tell the difference between a satin top and a tweed skirt,' she mumbled, all the huff sucked out of her.

He did the through-the-pupils stare. She could see his brain tick-ticking. 'And you always could, couldn't you? You just thought I wouldn't be able to keep it in my pants if you weren't wearing five-inch-thick flannel. Good old RJ, right?'

Up went her chin. 'When I came for my job interview I didn't know you had a harem of blonde bimbos at your disposal. And you...you can't deny it was a blessed relief to hire Miss Lemon! Finally someone you wouldn't be tempted to touch.'

'You know, for someone so smart...' He paced away, then back. 'I hired Catherine North—not her clothes. And I hired her because I liked what she had to say at her interview. She'd studied up on the industry and the company. She gave me an articulate rundown on the issues facing the

Australian property market. And when I asked her a question about our African development she ripped my head off on the subject of blood diamonds. The way you do that is one of the things I love—'

He ran a hand into his hair.

'I love that about you, Cathy. The way you think, the way you care. The way you make *me* think and care.' He shot her a fierce look. 'But by all means go and change into your tweed if it makes you feel safer!'

That ache in her chest was threatening to choke her. 'What's wrong with what I'm wearing, anyway?'

'Nothing,' Max said through his teeth, but he looked ready to throttle her. 'I just didn't think— Nothing.' And then, all tetchy, 'No, it's not nothing. You're not ready—so stop torturing me.'

'This is a perfectly respectable dress.'

'So respectable you were scared to wear it to work in Sydney?' Almost before he'd finished saying that, he had one of those *aha* moments. 'The only time you wore your real clothes was that day. The black top. When I wasn't supposed to be there.' Harsh laugh. 'No wonder you almost had a heart attack when I walked in. My God. *My. God.*'

His hands went digging into his hair.

'Well, Cathy, just to lay my cards on the table, you look gorgeous in that dress. You looked hot as hell last night. The night before, too. And don't get me started on the red peignoir. But I wanted you even in your atrocious skirts and your buttoned-up shirts and those chastity-belt cardigans.' He stepped closer. 'I am *not* your old boss, and I am *not* my father. A nice frock isn't going to push me over the edge.'

He took a furious step away. Another back.

'Get this though your head: it's not time until I say it is. No matter how high you up the ante.'

'Well, I am going to be upping it,' she said.

She took a step closer, until they were only a breath away from each other, and stared up at him. He looked down, shooting sparks.

His eyes dropped to her mouth.

*Do it...do it,* she urged silently.

The eyes dropped again, to her chest, and he licked his lips. She knew without looking that her nipples were erect, pointing through her dress.

'You can touch me if you want,' Catherine said.

The fire flared—hot and dangerous. And then his eyes shifted direction—to her earlobe—and one of her hands automatically reached up to her right ear, fondled the gold hoop there.

'Don't mind if I do,' Max said.

Catherine braced herself. Waiting for his hands to land... *where?*

But Max's hands stayed loose by his sides as he leaned down, nuzzled his nose, then his mouth, just below her left ear. He licked her there, the way she'd licked him last night. But longer, and with the flat of his tongue.

She couldn't hold in her shocked gasp as he moved fractionally, taking her earlobe into his mouth, complete with its gold hoop. His tongue was flicking at the same time as he suckled—and she was scared, so scared, she was going to fall apart.

And then he eased away. 'Your buttons have gone but you're still wearing the gold hoops, Cathy. And you know what that tells me? You're. Not. Ready. So stop poking the bear.'

One step away. Stop. Turn.

'And, Cathy—remember what I said. Touch another man and I'm out of the game. Not negotiable.' Sexy smile. 'Have a nice time tonight.'

Catherine blew out a long breath as he exited. Realised she was shaking.

*Lust.*

But not pure and simple.

There was something else there. Something...deeper.

She found that she was playing with her gold hoop again and stamped her foot so hard the heel snapped right off her shoe.

Max's dinner lasted fifty-seven minutes. He timed it, impatient for it to be over.

Not that the food wasn't great. The wine—excellent. Doug—his usual informative, sparkling self. But Max wanted to be somewhere else.

Where Cathy was.

*Yeah, she's with her date, moron! You do* not *want to be there.*

So—would the game be over tonight?

For reasons Max didn't want to examine, that thought made him furious.

By the time the car dropped him off at the resort he was so consumed by thoughts of some other guy hearing the sound of Catherine's breathy voice in his ear, feeling the tantalising promise of her tongue on his skin, he knew he wouldn't sleep.

He needed a drink. But, not being fit company for humans, he headed poolside, where the bar would soon close and he could be alone. Six minutes later he was swirling cognac in a balloon glass. It was a suitably brooding drink for his tortured state of mind. Meditative, soulful, pensive...

He laughed suddenly. He could almost *see* Cathy rolling her eyes should she get a look inside his head at that moment.

The last two swimmers got out of the pool, dried off and left. A minute later the barman closed up shop.

Alone.

Perfect.

He raised his glass to his lips and his eyes automatically focused on the balcony of the main hotel bar.

And then he saw them.

# CHAPTER TEN

MAX'S BLOOD ROCKETED through his veins. Hot, fast, painful.

Catherine. And Luke Phillips.

Options flashed through Max's mind. One—go to the bar, say a civil hello, subtly let her know their arrangement was at an end. Sane. Two—return to his cabin unseen, then tomorrow let her know their arrangement was at an end *not* so subtly. Sane. Three—spy on them and hold fire on declaring their arrangement at an end. *In*sane.

Which was how Max came to be edging his chair backwards, into the shadows, out of sight—half shielded for good measure by a palm tree. A freaking palm tree! Seriously? He tossed back the expensive cognac as if it was lemonade and trained his eyes on the balcony.

He could only see the top half of Catherine. But what he could see was beautiful. No glasses. Hair in a ponytail. Wearing something that completely covered her glorious chest, thank God! Nice and demure.

He switched to her companion. Luke Phillips. Alex Taylor black hair. Big warm smile. He was an inch or two shorter than Max—better for Catherine's height, Max *supposed*. He had a cleft in his chin—which for *some* reason women seemed to like.

Basically, Max wished Luke Phillips would drop dead.

Luke said something, making Catherine hoot out a laugh, and Max's eyes snapped back to her. What was so funny? And why didn't she ever, *ever* laugh like that with *him*?

And then Catherine picked up a glass—a shot glass!—raised it to her lips, and tossed its contents down as though she'd been frequenting bars since she was an infant.

Shots. They were doing *shots*.

Max, all gritted up, groaned low and fierce in the back of his throat as Catherine wiped the back of her hand over her mouth. He wanted to lick that sexy mouth of hers, suck the booze right out of her. Even if it turned out to be tequila—which he *hated*.

His stomach pitched as he saw Luke wave to one of the serving staff. A minute later the two of them were preparing to leave. So...Catherine would go back to her cabin and Luke would go home—*right*?

Max, on tenterhooks, scooted further back—so far back he was practically in the bushes!—because Catherine would walk past the pool to get to her cabin and he wasn't sure how he wanted to play things. Stay hidden? Or throw out a casual, *Hello, Cathy, how was your night?*—although how to make it casual, given he'd have to emerge from behind a palm tree, he wasn't sure. Maybe he would wait for her to get back to her cabin and then call her. Or maybe—

Maybe he could just instantaneously combust!

Because she was wearing shorts! *Tiny* shorts. And killer heels that looked amazing on her absolutely perfect legs. He wanted to run his hands, his mouth, up those legs, from the ankle to the hem, slide his tongue along her inner thigh...

Okay, if he didn't get it together he was going to end up being carted off in that strait-jacket she'd warned him about—and he wasn't even going to argue when they came to strap him in.

Catherine stopped Luke with a hand on his arm as they neared the pool. She stiffened, frowned, looked slowly around. And then, with a tiny head-shake, she turned back to Luke. 'You can't ride home in that state, Luke.'

Ride? Motorbike, then. Irresponsible lout. And *'that state'*? So—drunk. A motorbike-riding booze-hound. *Loser*.

'Stay in my cabin tonight,' she urged.

Max's jaw clamped so tightly as he waited for Luke's answer, he feared for the longevity of his two capped teeth—which, okay, were the result of a long-ago motorbike accident...*not* that the accident had been his fault!

He wasn't moving a tooth, a muscle or a limb from his spot until the bastard answered.

'Nah, I'm not staying,' Luke said. 'I'll want to kill you when I wake up sick as a dog to find *you* disgustingly bright-eyed and chirpy.'

'It's a good bet I'll wake up grumpy! I'm doing a lot of that.'

'Doesn't count if it's not from a hangover.' Luke glanced at the pool, mischief brewing in his eyes. 'Hey, Cath, remember that wedding? The one where those pretentious academics kept digging at you for being a "glorified secretary" instead of using your business degree? How I dared you to spice things up by jumping in the pool?'

'Yes—and I don't know what I was thinking! It cost me an expensive cocktail dress. Not to mention my favourite shoes.'

'You *weren't* thinking—you were in a rage. Like you've been most of the night. And that top you're wearing is cotton, not silk—right?'

'But these shorts are leather.'

Luke made clucking chicken noises.

'Oh, for God's sake, we really *are* regressing, aren't we? First shots—now this.' Catherine tried to sound disapproving, but ended up giggling. 'I'll do it. But only if you come in with me. And no shoes this time—even for *you* I won't ruin these!'

Luke simply started tugging off his footwear.

Catherine, leaning a hand on his shoulder, took care of hers. And then they smiled at each other.

Luke took her hand. 'Ready, Catherine-the-Great?'

'Ready!'

They ran. Jumped. Splashed into the pool with a shrieking whoop. And then they were laughing. Laughing, laughing, laughing as they splashed and dunked each other.

Eventually Catherine swam to the waterfall end of the pool, where it was shallow enough to stand. She waded to the side, hoisted herself onto the edge and sat with her legs dangling in the water.

'I have no idea what the point of that was, Luke—unless it was to sober me up.'

'Except that *I'm* the drunk one.' Luke hauled himself out of the pool and sat beside her. 'And the point is that I want you back, Catherine,' he said. 'I want *my* Catherine back.'

Catherine leaned against him, and for a long moment they sat staring into the water.

And then Catherine stiffened again.

'What is it?' Luke asked.

'Just that smell...'

Luke sniffed. 'It's nice. Like vanilla, but...darker.'

'Yes...' She looked around again. Peered into the shadows. And her eyes sharpened as she made out a form. 'Uh-oh.'

Luke swivelled and stared into the space.

A moment later Max walked out of the darkness.

Catherine got to her feet, streaming water. Luke followed her, standing close—*too* close—on Catherine's right. Catherine-the-Great, Luke had called her. *My Catherine.*

Max wondered what the hell he was going to do about that. He'd told her to find someone else, but he knew—very suddenly, very surely—he was not giving her up.

'Max, right?' Luke asked, with an unconcerned smile that made Max want to punch him.

'Right,' Max said, but he was looking at Catherine. That 'demure' top was clinging wetly to her, transparent. He could see her bra. Creamy, lacy half-cups, with her lovely breasts spilling over the top.

The curves everywhere else—luscious. The legs—insane! Everything about her was awesome. He was itching to touch her.

'Cath's been telling me about Kurrangii,' Luke said.

'Huh?'

'Kurrangii.'

Max transferred his gaze to Luke. 'Has she?'

Luke nodded a few too many times—the shots, no doubt. 'It sounds great.'

Silence.

Luke looked at Catherine, who was looking at Max.

'Cath, do you need me?' Luke asked.

She shook her head, eyes still on Max.

'Right, then.' Luke one-arm hugged Catherine, kissed the top of her wet head, walked over to his shoes and picked them up. He looked from Catherine to Max, back to Catherine. *'Okaaaaay,'* he said. 'I'm off. And don't freak, Cath, because I have a sober ride pre-arranged.'

He started to walk away, and Catherine seemed to come to her dazzled senses. 'Wait!' she called out, and hurried after him.

Max saw it as she turned. The tattoo. Through her transparent top.

At least he could see some of it. It was no modest little dolphin or flower or heart. It was big. It was bold. It looked like a falcon, and yet…not. He could see the part that stretched up the curve of her waist to just below her bra, but not the part that dipped below where her shorts rested enticingly on her hip. And, God, he wanted to see all of it. Every square millimetre. But he was *not* going to ask. Because she'd probably strip off and show him and then he would be lost.

Max watched as she hugged Luke, as they whispered something to each other. As Luke patted her back!

Max's mouth dropped open. Patted her *back*?

And then Luke was leaving, and Catherine was making her way slowly back.

'So, Max…' she said, and plucked her top away from her skin. Which did nothing except make Max realise he had enough material to fuel his wet dreams for the next twenty years. 'How long were you there, watching me?'

'Long enough,' he said, mouth dry.

She came closer. 'I could smell you, you know,' she said.

Man, oh, man, was that the most erotic thing he'd ever heard? Because it was making him bigger and harder than he'd ever been. And it was painful—but it felt so *good*.

She knew his scent.

He longed to invite her to stick her nose anywhere she wanted and breathe him in. But she wasn't ready. If he made his move before she was ready he would lose her. She would run. Hide somewhere else.

'Why were you watching me?' she asked.

At exactly the same time Max demanded, 'What's *wrong* with that guy, anyway?'

'That *guy*?' Catherine stepped closer. 'What makes you think there's *anything* wrong with "that guy"? Whose name is Luke—which you *know*, because you never forget a name.'

'He patted you on the back. When you hugged him.'

'And that would be bad as opposed to you lurking in the shadows watching me because…?'

'Because he'd have to be a eunuch to have you in his arms and not—' He stopped.

Another step. Closer.

'And not…?' she prompted.

Max stared down at her, wanting to grab her and shake her and kiss her and ban her from hugging any other man ever again. 'He didn't even look at you when you got out of the pool.'

Which was not exactly answering the question.

'So I have to tell you, I think—' Shrug. 'I think you could do better.'

Role reversal.

'You're giving me *dating* advice?' she asked with a low laugh.

Role reversal complete.

'Well, come on, Cathy. He didn't even *look* at you.' *Yeah, you said that already, mate.* 'And I mean—I mean *look* at you!'

'Why don't *you* look at me?' Very low, very husky.

'I am.'

She stepped back. Opened her arms wide, stuck out her spectacular breasts. 'I mean *really* look.'

Okay, he looked. Really looked. Hard. Well, she'd told him to, hadn't she?

'Do you like what you see?' she asked.

He closed his eyes for a brief, get-it-together moment. Then opened them, keeping them safely on her face this time as he crossed his arms and secured his hands safely under his armpits.

'You know I do, Catherine. Because I'm not a eunuch. And I'm a little over being a saint right now, too.'

'I don't want a saint.' Small smile. 'Because *I'm* not a saint.'

'Yeah, I got that—if you were a saint you wouldn't be torturing me.'

'My brother, Luke, thinks I should torture you a little more.'

That took Max a moment to process. *Brother?* 'No. His name is Phillips.'

'See? You never forget a name. Half-brother—hence the different surname. But still brother. Which is why he didn't look at me the way you're looking at me.' She moved closer. 'So if it's the thought of Luke that's stopping you…'

Max swallowed, hard. *Not ready. She wasn't ready.* Teeth grinding. Hands fisting in his armpits. Heart hammering. It took the black spots spinning in front of his eyes to remind him to breathe.

She stepped closer still, and Max momentarily lost his mind. Lost control of his body, too. Because his arms had uncrossed and closed around her like a vice. And then he was dragging her onto her toes and kissing her, *devouring* her. In an endless stream of succulent, licking kisses, pausing only to breathe before planting his mouth on hers again. Tequila. She tasted like tequila. He *loved* tequila. Tequila was his favourite drink.

Okay. He was officially insane. Strait-jacket required.

He pulled back, breaths choppy and desperate, looked down at her. 'Okay, you win. You wanted to push me until I couldn't stop and I'm there. I can't stop.'

'You *will* stop, Max, if I ask. I know you will.'

He looked down at her, torn. God, how was he going to pull back?

'But I'm *not* asking you to,' she said steadily. 'I don't want you to stop.'

The words spurred him almost to madness. He was shaking as he kissed her again, backing her into the darkness. Back, back, back, until she was against the palm tree. Thank *God* for that palm tree. Mouth on hers—hungry, desperate. Hands reaching for her breasts through that damp top—too rough, but he couldn't seem to be gentle. Clenching, massaging. He could feel the points of her nipples against his palms.

Catherine moaned into his mouth, pushing herself more fully into his hands. His knee was between her thighs, urgent against the core of her.

'I want you in my mouth...here,' he said, rolling her nipples. 'To be inside you...' He nudged his thigh more closely against the juncture of her thighs.

'Do it. Take me. Right here—now.'

With a groan, Max lowered his head to suck her through the material of her top, the lacy bra beneath. He was holding her breasts in his hands, raising them for his tongue, fingers manipulating them out of the cups of her bra. He was so hot for her he thought he might explode. She'd told him to take her. So he would take.

Hands shaking, mouth seeking, fingers delving, he heard...felt...the gossamer-thin fabric tear.

Then Catherine's voice, low and urgent in his ears. '*Don't* stop, Max. Take me.'

And the sound of her words, the echo of the ripping fabric, coalesced in his head and he froze. Long, *long* moment. He could hear his breath surging in and out, the silent scream of his body as he raised his head. Then he moved his thigh, drew it out from between hers. Disengaged. Stepped back.

She was staring at him, all wide eyes and swollen mouth. Her top was torn over her right breast, the bra showing, her nipple visible over the top of the cup. Shuddering at the gorgeous, wanton sight of it, Max had to close his eyes. He'd never heard of anyone coming just from looking at someone, but there was always a first time and he felt perilously close to it.

With quickly efficient movements he stripped off his shirt, offered it to her.

She shook her head.

'Put it on, Catherine. Secluded or not, we're outside. Anyone could walk past.'

She waited…indecisive. And then, with a muffled exclamation, she wrenched the shirt from him, shoved her arms into the sleeves, yanked it closed over her chest.

'Don't say sorry,' Catherine said, and ran a shaky hand over her hair—which he must have loosened in that mad scramble, because it was a mess. 'I wanted that as much as you did.'

'Then why didn't you touch me?'

'But I *did*!' Part cry, part plea.

'You let *me* touch *you*. Very different proposition. My tongue was everywhere in your mouth. Where was yours? Not in *my* mouth! Your hands—down by your sides. While mine were all over you. Well, I don't want to *take* you, Cathy. This should not be about *taking*.'

'It was just an expression. The taking thing.'

'No, it wasn't. I think this whole thing is about you wielding the power that was stolen from you. Because you're so sure I'll stop if you tell me to. And when you say stop—and I *do* stop—you know you're in control. But you make me so maddened with lust even *I* don't know if I'll stop. For one moment there I was on the brink, believe me. And I tore your top, Cathy! Remind you of anyone? Can you see what's happening to me? Because I can. And I *hate* it.'

Catherine was doing up the buttons on his shirt with fumbling fingers. 'You're not like him.'

'Then stop punishing me. That's what you're doing when you hold yourself back. Because I can't have what I want until you're ready. And it's unbearable. Why do you want to punish me? Because you can't get to *him*? Or is this about seeing if I'll snap and *be* him? Because I will *not* be him.'

'I—I just—I just want to get over...get over...' She seemed unable to find the words, and in the end let out a muffled scream of frustration and turned her back on him.

'I get it, Cathy,' he said softly. 'I've been your safe haven, your hideout, ever since you came for that job interview in your camouflage gear, so scared that even a *hint* of uncardiganed flesh would have me snuffling after your body fluids.'

'I'm not in camouflage gear any more.'

'And, believe me, I've felt every nanosecond of the slow striptease. But I wanted you before you took out the first hairpin. You're just icing a cake I already wanted to sink my teeth into.'

She spun back round. 'So sink your teeth in. I'm here. Ready, willing.'

'Just not able. And I am *not* giving you an excuse to run away and hide again.' Max rubbed his hands over his face. 'Now I'm going to bed.'

He saw the look on her face and held up his hand.

'Alone. You're going to have to wait a little longer, passion flower. You still have quite a bit of unfurling to do.' And then he sighed. 'More's the pity.'

Catherine tossed and turned. Got up, went back to bed, got up, went back to bed, got up. Finally she walked onto the deck, staring into the darkness of the river, trying to soak up some of its peace.

Max saw inside her head better than she did. Her need to feel safe, her need to punish him—and herself, too. Her need to push Max to breaking point to prove he wasn't RJ—or perhaps that he...*was*? Her need to run. Hide. Bury herself so she was safe.

And that meant she was still in gaol. Her beautiful phoenix tattoo was just ink in her skin—not a symbol of her rise from the ashes of the past. Her clothes were just textiles over flesh—the old clothes hadn't protected her; the news ones weren't freeing her. Was there even any point to *Passion Flower* if her alter ego Jennifer's freedom to touch and be touched by the man she wanted stayed stubbornly on the page?

It started to rain—one drop, then a few more. More, more—until it was sluicing through the trees in sheets, thumping the river's surface. Catherine felt moisture on her face. Cheeks, mouth. She licked. Tasted salt. Tears, not rain. *Tears.*

Tears for the passion flower whose petals had been so comprehensively plucked, she'd stood like a denuded stem in Max's arms. Her tongue securely in her own mouth. Melting with lust when he put his hands on her breasts but choking the whimpers back. Desperate to rock herself on that thigh he'd shoved against her but standing still. Wanting to slide her hand over his beautiful, bare, bronzed chest when he'd given her his shirt...but buttoning the shirt over her own chest instead.

*'I don't want to take you.'*

She straightened her shoulders. At least in *Passion Flower* she could make him take her. She could do whatever she wanted. Alex and Jennifer at the palm tree, Alex staring into her eyes, saying, *'Yes, Jenny, I will take you, and you will be mine...'*

Catherine woke late the next morning, having written and then dreamed herself into a state of unbridled lust.

She scrambled into the first dress she could lay her hands on, yanked her hair into a ponytail, jammed on her glasses, grabbed her work folders and left the room just as her usual maid, Emily, arrived to clean the cabin. Which meant she really was cutting it fine!

She hurried along the path, flicking through her folders... *Damn!* One missing. Going back for it would make her late for the first time in her life and Max would probably think she was scared to face him or something equally pathetic. Galling—but there wasn't much she could do about it except hurry.

She removed her shoes so she could run, and regretted it as she *ouch-ouched* her way along the pebble-strewn path and padded up the steps to her cabin. She was going to have to wait for a buggy to get to the meeting, which would make her even later, because her feet couldn't take another bruising run.

She whooshed through her door, and any thought of buggies and feet flew straight out of her head. It took her only a moment to process the scene—young, tiny Emily, pinned to the bed by a man wearing a manager's uniform—before she advanced, roaring, flinging her files and her shoes at the man's bulky back.

He rolled off Emily and lurched to his feet, cursing.

'What the *hell* do you think you're doing?' Catherine demanded.

He set his jaw. 'This is none of your business.'

Catherine goggled at him. 'A woman being raped on *my* bed is none of my business?'

With a threatening look at Emily, who'd scrambled off the bed and was adjusting her uniform, he started hurrying towards the door.

Catherine rushed ahead to block his exit. 'Oh, no, you don't. And don't waste your warning looks on Emily. *I'm* the one who's going to cook your goose.'

'It's not what you think…' he blustered.

'Well—' quick peer at his name badge '—Raymond, tell me what it *is*.'

'A consultation. I'm her boss.'

'And do you consult with your *male* staff while lying on top of them?'

'It was consensual,' Raymond said, and tried again to leave.

Catherine laughed in his face and Raymond grabbed her,

trying to push her out of his way. Up went her right knee—reflex. A graze, not a direct hit, because Raymond was still in motion. But although he stayed on his feet he'd lost any semblance of control. He grabbed Catherine by her ponytail, using it to shove her into the doorjamb.

She felt a sting near her eyebrow, heard a crack. Grappling. Cursing. Emily crying…racing across the room. Shove, shove, scuffle.

A rush, a flash—and Raymond was racing down the wooden steps.

Sobbing, Emily threw herself into Catherine's arms.

Max checked his watch again—not even pretending to listen to his Queensland manager Eric's presentation on state tourism partnerships.

Where the hell *was* she?

Too angry about last night to be in the same room as him?

He couldn't blame her—his own body had vented its fury on him by throbbing all night long. But Catherine was a confronter, not an avoider—it was one of the things he loved about her. No way would she hide in her cabin.

So…hungover? She hadn't seemed drunk, but those *were* tequila shots she'd been drinking.

Or… An accident? Max felt his pulse surge.

He shoved his chair back from the table. Eric stopped. Max stood—and then the door opened. And she was there.

Max let out a slow, shaky breath as he slid back into his seat.

'I'm sorry—an emergency,' Catherine said, and hurriedly took her seat.

Eric, with a nervous look at Max, picked up where he'd so suddenly left off.

And Max continued not to listen. Instead he watched Catherine out of the corner of his eye. Her fingers were trembling. There was a scratch at the end of her eyebrow. A break in the tortoiseshell frame of her glasses.

What the hell had happened?

Max shoved his chair back again. Eric stopped again. Max gathered his work.

'Sorry, everyone, I have a conference call. Eric—you're all right to take over? Good. I'll see you at lunch. Cathy? I need you.'

Catherine picked up her folders and followed Max from the room. 'What call?' she asked as he flagged down a buggy.

'No call,' Max said. 'We're going to my cabin so you can tell me what's happened.'

'But—'

Max held up a 'stop' hand. 'Hate. That. Word.'

He waited until Catherine was seated in the buggy, then got in beside her, conscious that her trembling was systemic, feeling it even though they weren't touching.

Once inside his cabin, he poured her a glass of water, set it on the coffee table, gestured for her to sit on the couch.

'Okay?' he asked.

She nodded.

'Then tell me.'

Catherine opened her mouth.

And burst into tears.

# CHAPTER ELEVEN

So...HANDKERCHIEF, RIGHT?

Max patted his pocket hopefully, but didn't know why. He wasn't a handkerchief kind of guy.

Tissues, then. She needed tissues.

He bounded into the bathroom, grabbed the tissue box, bounded back. Stood there ineffectually. Then, with a hand-in-hair-because-I-have-no-idea-what-I'm-doing gesture, he sat beside her. He ripped a firestorm of tissues from the box and handed the wad to her. Then he gave in to impulse, tucked her under his arm, drew her against his side.

And waited.

Until the sobs became hiccups. Until the hiccups became a series of sighing breaths. Until the sighing breaths settled.

'So, *not* a hangover?' he asked, trying to lighten the atmosphere.

Catherine did a weird laugh/snort combo. 'No. I could drink you and ten of your friends under the table.'

'No way.'

'Way.'

'So you weren't drunk last night?'

'I wasn't exactly sober. Why else would I jump into the hotel pool wearing leather?'

Leather. The shorts. Max had to grit his teeth as the memory of her in those shorts whacked him in the groin.

He shook his head to clear it. 'So...?'

'What happened?' she asked, and *shuddered.* 'Raymond.'

The hairs on the back of Max's neck rose. All because of a man's name. He had the first inkling that he was in trouble here. Big trouble.

'Going to need more,' he said.

'Sexual harassment,' she said.

Cold, murderous rage. Like an icy spear through the brain. He concentrated on his heartbeat, trying to contain it.

'He touched you?'

Catherine angled her head to look up at him. Smiled—not that Max knew what there was to smile at—then reached up a hand, touched his cheek so gently, as though he were the one needing comfort.

'Not me, Max. It won't be me ever again. Okay?'

The relief was so huge Max felt light-headed with it. He grabbed her hand, kissed it, held it on his lap. He couldn't seem to take his eyes off it, resting there on his thigh, looking...*right*. So right he had trouble concentrating on what she was saying about being late, forgetting something, seeing Emily on the bed. Raymond.

The name echoed in his head. *Raymond.*

'...tried to stop him.'

Okay—he'd missed something important. 'Stop him?'

Catherine nodded. 'I knew those self-defence classes would come in handy.'

Max looked at her blankly.

'I took self-defence classes after...after.'

He felt a weird melting sensation around his heart. Amazing that he could get all twisted up over the fact that a woman had learned how to take a man down. But it was just so... her. So *her*.

'Yeah, of course you did,' he said, and heard the smile in his voice. *Big* trouble. 'So you did...what?'

'Kneed him,' she said. 'You know, like...*kneed* him.' She was looking at him, wide-eyed and proud. 'In the groin.'

'You go, girl,' Max said, and kissed the top of her head.

'It *did* feel good,' she admitted, relaxing against him.

'But it wasn't a direct hit. Which is how he managed to grab me and— Ouch!'

Max let go of her suddenly crunched hand. 'He *what*?'

'He grabbed my hair. Like this—' She grabbed her ponytail, pulled it. 'Ouch!' she said again.

'What happened next?'

He could hear the barely tethered danger in his voice but it seemed Catherine could not, because she answered with a nonchalant wave of her hand—a still trembling hand, which edged his anger higher.

'He...what? Waved a hand at you?'

'No, Max, he didn't wave a *hand* at me!'

That sounded tetchy, which gave Max a level of comfort.

'He shoved me into the doorjamb. And now I'm going to need new glasses.' She took off her glasses, looked mournfully at the broken frame.

As gently as he could—which wasn't easy because he'd never felt so violent—Max tilted her face so he could see the gash near her eyebrow. 'I'll call for a doctor.'

'What is it with you and doctors?' Catherine asked, flicking her chin from his grasp. 'Next thing you'll be tucking me into bed with a hot toddy.'

Bed. *His* bed. So close. Cathy naked in it.

Max tried to block the image but it was there, like a beacon, flashing at him. *Take me, take me now, take me.*

Oblivious, Catherine was prodding at her wound. 'I put some antiseptic on it. That'll do. Emily was in worse shape— not physically, but emotionally. God knows what would have happened if I hadn't burst in when I did.'

Okay—limit reached!

Max jumped to his feet, started pacing, needing an outlet for his dark energy. 'Something *did* happen, Catherine! He *hurt* you.' Stop. Glare. 'What were you thinking, to be taking that guy on?'

Catherine jammed her glasses back on. 'What is *wrong* with you?' She jumped to *her* feet. Stripping the elastic from her hair, she started pacing in the opposite direction from him, winding her hair round and round in an approximation of a chignon. 'Someone had to help her. And I *told* you I had a punishing right knee—my aim was just a little off this time. And you seemed to think my knee action was admirable a few minutes ago.'

'Yes, but—but— God.' Stop. Glare. 'You should have let him go and called me.'

Stop. Glare. 'Oh, really? So you could come and save the day? I thought Sir Galahad was flipping burgers with Elvis!' She started securing her hair with the elastic, doubling, tripling it around the tight bun with a snap. 'I know all about men saving the day. I'll look after myself, thank you.'

'What does *that* mean?'

'Who do you think stood by doing nothing while my boss was attacking me?'

'Who?'

'My boyfriend—that's who!' Catherine walked right up to Max, still glaring. 'The man I was stupid enough to follow to the Middle East.'

And then the fight seemed to go out of her. And he hated that. *Hated* it. Wanted to hug her again. What *was* that, with the hugging?

Catherine ran a hand over her eyes. 'No point talking about him. It's over.'

Well, whatever the hugging thing was, Max couldn't seem to help it. He pulled her into his arms. He heard, *felt* the sob as she buried her face there, and it almost broke his heart.

'It's *not* over, Cathy. You're not over it. And I need to know so I have some clue how to stop sticking my foot in my mouth up to the patella.'

Long, fraught silence. And then she nodded. Just once, against his chest. 'All right. You can let me go. I'm not going to cry.'

'I'm not letting you go, Cathy. I'll never let you go. Get used to that idea and things will be a lot easier.'

He felt a shiver race through her. 'You will. When the time comes. And it won't make you like your father. It won't be your fault. It will be mine—for writing the book that started everything unravelling on Friday night, for pushing you ever since.'

His arms tightened. 'Cathy, can't you see? I've been putting myself wherever you were every chance I could so you *could* push me. I *wanted* you to push me. I wanted you to push me until we were in it up to our necks. God knows why, but that's where we are.'

There was a long silence.

And then she spoke. 'James—that's his name—kept telling me I was imagining things. When it became clear that I wasn't imagining *anything*, that it was real and happening to me—*me*!—when I'd always been so scathing of women who put up with such behaviour, had been so sure I never would—' She choked there.

Max forced himself not to tense, just to hold her. Safe, protected.

'James said... He said I could handle it,' she said. 'And I was arrogant enough to believe it. When it escalated I wanted to go to Human Resources and report it, but James begged me not to because he'd got me the job and it wouldn't look good for him. That's love for you! Back then I really didn't know the score—but James sure taught me.'

She pulled away, gave him a smile so brittle he felt his heart crack.

'And you're so right, Max. An endless stream of just-sex-no-forever is a lot less painful than promising love.'

'Cathy, we both know I say some stupid things. Don't throw them at me.'

'I need... I need space. The river. It's...soothing.'

She opened the doors, stepped onto the deck, waited for Max to join her. 'You know what really gets me?' she asked. 'That James used the things he supposedly loved about me to make me "behave". I was *feisty*, I was *fearless*, I never took crap from *anyone*—so why couldn't I handle one man?'

She raised her hands to her mouth, breathed through them for a moment. Then she squared her shoulders, dropped her hands to her sides. 'In D.C., it became clear that I could *not* handle that one man and I was frightened. I didn't bother calling James that last time, since he clearly couldn't have cared less about me. I called the head of HR instead. HR— responsible for staff welfare, right? *Wrong.* Because our head of HR *advised* me that it would be dangerous for someone in my position—someone secretly living in an *illegal* unmarried state with a man—to make trouble in Abu Najmah. Because it would only take one phone call and I'd be arrested. Funny, isn't it? My boss sexually harasses me, but *I* could be the one arrested.'

She shifted restlessly.

'So I sat in my hotel room, wondering what it was about me that made my boyfriend think it was okay to essentially prostitute me. That made my boss think he could feel me up whenever the urge took him. That made HR tell me to shut up about it.' She was shaking with anger as she turned to him. 'Better to look after myself, don't you think, with that track record? Like I did today.'

Max raised a hand to touch her but Catherine pulled away.

'Keep your sympathetic pats,' she said. 'Just help me. Have sex with me, Max. Take away all those terrible memories and give me new ones. *Now.*'

'When you're ready,' he said, and it came out harshly.

She whirled to the river, tore the elastic from her hair and threw it in. Next the little gold hoops were ripped from her ears, hurled at the water. She spun back to him. Vibrating with rage. Glowing with it. Magnificent. 'Well, I'm not hanging around waiting for you to get it up. So screw you, Maximilian Rutherford! Screw. *You.*'

'Nice choice of words,' he said mildly.

'I've got others! Plenty.'

'Oh, I'm sure you do. You know, I *always* knew there was something under that prim and proper exterior. I just didn't know the extent. And now, at last, the real, full-strength Catherine North makes an appearance. *Bravo.*'

'And you're not man enough for her,' Catherine sneered.

'You won't like the real Catherine North. She swears. She drinks. She has a tattoo. She skinny-dips, she bungee-jumps and sky-dives, and she rides a motorbike like her brother and her tattooed-freak neighbour. She is *not* a virgin. In fact she once had sex in a movie theatre.'

'I'll see your movie theatre and raise you a department store women's fitting room. You're not scaring me, Cathy. Now, anything else you'd like to get out of your system while we're going?'

'I'm done. I resign.'

'No. You don't.'

'I do.'

He grabbed her arms. 'Every time you threaten to leave I know you're not ready. I'm not letting you run and hide, Cathy.'

'It's not running if there's nothing to run *from*.'

'What about a job you're good at? And what about me?'

'There are other jobs. And other bosses. Maybe even one who won't have to be coerced into taking me to bed. So from here on in you can shove your "poor little Cathy" sentiments right up your—'

Max jerked her in, kissed her hard on the mouth before she could get that suggestion out of her mouth. And then, past bearing it another second, he spun her to face the river. He'd give her *soothing*! He bent her forward, hiked up the back of her dress.

'Is that better?' he demanded. 'Do you really want me to use you like he did? You want me to snap? Well, I'm snapping. I'm done. I'm going to take you, Catherine. Right now, on this deck.' He was breathing hard in her ear, his arms like steel bands around her. 'Now, test me a little more. Tell me to stop. Will I or won't I, do you think?'

She kept her mouth closed but her body was rigid.

'Come on, Cathy.' He thrust against her bottom.

'No,' she said, and the word sounded torn out of her. 'I'm not going to say it.'

He used his chin to nudge her hair away from her neck. Put his mouth there and sucked hard, *hard*, until she cried out.

'I want you so much I'm shaking with it. Can you feel it? *Can* you?'

'Yes—yes!' she panted.

'But you know what, passion flower? I *am* going to stop.'

Another sucking kiss, a tortured groan against her skin. And then slowly, painfully, he pulled away. He reefed her around to face him, jerked her hem down.

'And now we know,' he said.

'Now we know *what*?'

'That I'm not like RJ. And I'm not like my father. And I sure as hell am not like your loser ex-boyfriend. Because I won't hurt you, and I won't use you, and I won't let anyone else do it, either.'

There were tears in her eyes. 'I already knew that.'

'But I didn't, Cathy. *I* didn't.'

'So now you know and now I know. Finish it.'

'No.'

She stared at him. Incredulous. Furious. Sexy as hell.

'Are you serious? You're really and truly *stopping*?'

'Just because you say yes doesn't make it right. You're not ready.'

'You—you—you—'

'Careful, firebrand. Don't say something you'll regret.'

Foot-stomp with a hair-toss thrown in. 'You are *not* leaving me like this!'

Max snatched her into his arms again. He was half laughing, half groaning as he hugged her. Kissed her mouth hard. Then the top of her head. 'Yes, Cathy, I am leaving. Because I have to make sure Raymond is dealt with—and don't bother telling me you can look after that yourself.'

'I *can* look after it myself, damn you.'

'Then I'm going to the business lunch you arranged—don't come.'

'I'm coming.'

Another laugh. 'Tell you what, Cathy, come or not to the

afternoon meetings. But nudge my leg just once under the table and you'll know all about *coming*. And in front of all those business people! Got it?'

Catherine wondered if Max could hear the echo of her, *'Arrgggggghhhhhh!'* as he strode up the path. Because it had disturbed a whole array of birdlife.

She raked her hands through her hair, yanking it.

'Ouch!'

That didn't help.

So she took off her damaged glasses, threw them on the wooden deck and stamped on them.

That didn't help, either.

*'Arrgggggghhhhhh!'*

There went the birds again.

What the hell was going on in his head? Because she just didn't get it.

Max wanted her. She could *feel* it—she could almost taste it. He'd been huge and hot and shaking. He'd given her a love-bite. Who over the age of sixteen *did* that without a total loss of control?

How many times did she have to ask? To beg? To—?

*Oh.*

It was there—the answer—shimmering like a promise.

Catherine-the-Great did not ask and beg. She did not submit. She didn't *allow* a man to kiss her, to touch her, acting like a block of damned *wood*.

*That* was what Max was waiting for. For her to be in it. *Up to her neck.*

If she wanted him to take her she had to take *him*.

Well. All right, then.

It didn't take long for Max, in full wrath of God mode, to get Raymond sorted.

Getting himself sorted was another matter.

He was a mess. A lust-crazed, desperate, testosterone-laden mess. He wanted her so damned *much*.

Catherine-the-Great, her brother had called her.

And she was.

She'd said she wouldn't allow RJ Harrow to be the yard-stick by which she measured every sexual relationship for the rest of her life and she'd shown her mettle—coming after him, bold and beautiful, to prove it. How could you not love that?

Defiant. Brave. Smart. Tough and feisty and sexy and outrageous. She could make him laugh and steam and want and pant. Every feeling he had for her was over the top. She was everything any man would want. His for the taking. He'd never wanted a woman more.

And he was going to have her.

Just as soon as he'd worked out how to keep her.

Because the way she kept trying to resign did not fill him with confidence.

If she left there would be a huge, gaping hole. How would he ever fill it?

*By getting yourself a tall, horsey blonde, idiot.*

He could just hear Catherine saying that—and the fact that it made him laugh out loud, in the middle of the guy next to him at the lunch table telling him about a failed de-velopment in the Northern Territory—*not* funny—had him seriously wondering about that strait-jacket.

Had she cooled down yet? He doubted it. He was sure he could anticipate some revenge for the way he'd left her. Like wearing something to the afternoon meetings designed to drive him wild. Touching him in some oh-so-innocent way, expressly to fry him a little hotter.

And the weird thing was he was looking forward to it.

He took his seat in the meeting room after lunch with a feeling of anticipation way out of proportion to what was on the agenda, watching as each participant arrived, wait-ing for her. Waiting. Waiting…

By start time everyone was seated—except her. But he knew she wouldn't have been able to resist that 'come or not' dare he'd flung at her—so he delayed the start of the meeting. She'd arrive at any moment. Any moment now. Any moment...

Fifteen minutes past start time Catherine's seat remained defiantly empty.

And Max wanted to punch something!

He caught one or two curious looks and knew he could wait no longer. 'Okay, let's start,' he said, and wrenched his folder open. Blindly, he pulled out whatever was on top.

And shock stopped his breath with the first word: *Jennifer.*

*Jennifer was waiting. Perfectly poised. Candlelit. Wearing something white and floaty. The music oozed, slow and steady, as she held out her arms, the white shifting and flowing around her body...*

*Oh. My. God.* Max looked down at his lap. Yep. Straight to attention down there.

He shoved the pages back into the folder. 'Right. Er... Right. Where we were?'

The meeting progressed, but Max's brain disengaged and every time his voice wasn't actually needed he slyly opened the folder—just enough for him to read secretly.

*'One rule,' Jennifer whispered. 'Say you'll agree or this goes no further.'*

*'I promise. Anything—anything at all.'*

*'No touching, Alex. The only one touching tonight is me...'*

Max shoved his chair back—there didn't seem to be room for his legs *and* his hard-on under the table—then shoved it straight back in before anyone clapped eyes on his lap.

'Problem, Max?' Eric asked.

Max wondered if he looked as if he was about to come. Because that was what he felt like.

'No—no problem,' Max said, sounding strained. 'Just—
Nothing. Continue.'

*Stop reading.*

But as they moved on to the next topic Max—almost pa-
thetically grateful at being able to hand the floor to Doug
for a PR round-up—opened his folder again.

*She swirled around him, hands smoothing across his
chest. Another swirl and she was leaning over him,
breasts tantalisingly close to his mouth.*

*'There are seven veils, Alex. And they're coming off
one by one before your blue, blue eyes. By the time the
last one hits the floor you'll be inside me...'*

Blue-eyed Alex. Him. Inside her. *Him.*

*Okay. Okay, okay, okay—calm down. Calm the hell down.*

But he couldn't calm own.

By the time the meeting broke up Max's heart had been
going hard enough and long enough to constitute an aero-
bic workout.

He went back to his cabin. Took a cold shower. Undid
the scant good the shower had done him by reading the
scene again.

It was game over.

He couldn't walk around with his hands jammed under
his armpits for the rest of his life, trying not to touch her.
So he was going to touch—and he was going to make it so
damned good she'd sign her life away for more.

He was experienced with women. Successful in business. A shrewd entrepreneur used to getting his own way.
A natural and efficient problem-solver.

One short, prim, *im*proper brunette was not going to get
the better of him.

It was time to take control.

First he would give her a little of her own medicine and
make sure he looked as hot as a forest fire for tonight's
dinner.

Then, after dinner, they would have a civilised discussion about how their affair was going to proceed—the ground rules for managing the affair and a suitable salary package that would contract her to Rutherford Property for an unbreakable term irrespective of anything personal that happened between them.

Then he would take her to bed.

He was whistling as he headed to the restaurant, alive with the need to see Catherine, ready to seal the deal.

But Catherine wasn't there.

She'd certainly *been* there. The *maître d'* had been given exhaustive instructions—and he showed Max a checklist to prove it. Place cards were precisely placed. Flowers, music, lighting had been adjusted to her specifications. The wines had been tasted. Everything was perfect.

But no Catherine.

She didn't show. Not once.

And Max was going to wring her damned neck!

He'd have to find her first, he realised, when his frantic knocking on her cabin door elicited no response.

He headed back to his cabin. If he was going to lose his marbles he'd do it in privacy, with a copy of *Passion Flower* in one hand and his phone in the other, with Catherine's number on constant redial.

He was so focused on his plan, the muted glow of lights didn't register straight away as he entered his cabin and reached for the light switch.

And then...

'Don't.'

# CHAPTER TWELVE

CATHY.

He turned into the room. Saw candles set around the room. Soft. Romantic.

One chair in the middle of the space.

He swallowed. Hard.

Music started. Sultry, oozing.

And then she was there. Framed by the doors that opened onto the deck. Dressed in white. Gauzy swathes of white.

Her face was covered, and yet not covered, by a sheer veil. He could make out her hair, dark and heavy and loose. His fingers twitched with the need to touch it.

'You read it?' she asked, just audible above the sensual flow of the music.

He nodded, mute.

She smiled. 'Then you know what to do. Sit.' One hand, imperious, emerged from the white.

Max sat like the slave he was. *Her* slave. He'd do anything for her.

She posed in the doorway. A heartbeat. Two. Then she came swaying sinuously towards him, in time with the beat.

Max's heart was hammering. She was a step away, just one, when she removed the veil covering her face and dropped it onto his lap.

She'd darkened her eyelids. Smudgy. Mysterious. Beautiful. She leaned in close and he couldn't stop himself—he reached to touch that swinging hair.

With a low, throaty laugh, Catherine stepped out of reach. 'Can't be trusted, can you?'

She snatched the white veil off his lap.

'Don't put it back on, Cathy. I want to see your face,' Max said.

'Oh, I'm not putting it back on. All these veils are coming off. Every last one of them.' She leaned close again and the waft of her perfume made him moan. 'But if I can't trust you not to touch...'

She moved behind him, caught his hands, looped them together with the white silk. And then she swirled in front of him again. Removed one more swathe of white, dropped it on the floor at his feet.

Five veils to go.

She went swirling away, sinuous as a snake.

Max could make out the shape of her body beneath the veils. See the shape and jut of her nipples. The hazy dark triangle at the juncture of her thighs. If just that vague darkness had him groaning with need how was he going to last? He wasn't. Not going to last. *Not.* He'd be coming like a schoolboy before she got the last veil off.

And then she was back, beside his chair, so close. She undid his shirt buttons, spread the shirt open. She slid her palms over his pectoral muscles. A little hesitant, tentative, at first—then growing bolder as he sat tied, panting. Her fingers swept across his nipples, stilled. Then she smiled, hands moving down his ribs. She leaned in close, licked one nipple, sucked it into her mouth.

Max jumped—and the chair jumped with him. 'Untie me.'

One more lick, and then she stood. Said, 'No.' Dropped a veil at his feet.

Four to go.

And away she went, dancing towards the deck.

She stopped there, turned. Started sliding her way back to him. He couldn't even blink. Didn't want to miss a split-second. Because he knew what she was going to do next...

Then she was there, turning her back to him, backing up

to him. Swaying, swaying, swaying those hips as she did it. Lowering, lowering, hovering just above his lap. He could feel the heat of her, smell the muskiness of her arousal. She went just low enough to wriggle an amateur lap dance— sexier than anything he'd experienced in his misspent young adulthood in gentlemen's clubs. He could just make out the flesh beneath the white, from below her gorgeous hair down to her backside. Could see the shape of the vivid tattoo he was so wild to know. The scent, the warmth, the sight of her, caused his hips to rise of their own volition, trying to connect with her.

'No,' she said, and danced away.

'Untie me, Cathy.'

'No.'

One more veil dropped.

Three to go.

And now he could clearly make out her nipples. She couldn't have missed the pinging direction of his gaze.

Next moment she was taking her breasts in her hands, pinching the nipples through the veil. 'Do you want me?' she asked.

He nodded. 'Dying.'

She smiled and came back to him. Reached for the buttons of his pants. One, two, three, four. Spread the fly, ran her hands over the length of him.

The chair jumped again, with him on it.

'I'm going to take you in my mouth soon,' she said. 'But first...' She reached inside his underwear and a groan of almost anguished pleasure was ripped out of his throat.

'Untie me,' he demanded. 'I have to touch you, Cathy.'

Instead, hands still fondling him, Catherine leaned in and kissed him. Hard and soft. Slanting, eager. Kissing, then retreating. Licking. Retreating. Whenever her mouth connected with his Max ground his lips onto hers, tongue thrusting, lashing. Hot, eager, desperate.

Then—gone. She was gone again. And Max sat rigid, so ready for her he thought he might actually cry.

One more veil was tossed to the floor.

Two left.

And now he could see her clearly through the fabric. Every lush curve. Every shadow. The dash of dark hair he was dying for. Nipples pink and perfect.

Oooohhh, God help him. She was coming back.

Before he could mentally prepare she was in front of him, kneeling at his feet, tugging his pants and underwear down to his ankles. But it wasn't much of a relief to have his erection springing out when he couldn't do anything with it.

All he could do was watch as she leaned forward, took him in her mouth. His eyes rolled back in his head and his teeth clenched as his hips bucked once, twice, three times.

'Cathy,' he said, 'I swear I am going to come.'

She glanced up at him. Wicked. Teasing. 'What's wrong with that?'

'I want to be inside you when I do.'

She laughed—that throaty, taunting sound—got to her feet and danced away.

'Two left, Max.'

'Rip them off. *Now*, for God's sake.'

With one whooshing move the second to last veil was gone—and her breasts were bare. He stared. Big, round, high, creamy. The generous areolae seemed swollen. Her nipples were pink and tight, and he wanted them in his mouth more than he wanted to breathe. Was his tongue lolling? Very likely. But he didn't have the sanity required to shove it back inside his mouth.

She came back to him. Yanked his shirt off his shoulders as far as she could with the impediment of the chair and his bound wrists. He could only sit there, salivating.

And then she was rubbing her breasts over his chest. He could feel the satin of her skin, the sharp peaks. He was going out of his mind.

'Aren't you going to watch?' she asked.

'If I open my eyelids my eyeballs are going to explode. That's what the pressure is like inside my head.'

Another warm slide of her breasts and then—nothing. He felt, *heard* her step back. He was damned sure it still wasn't safe to open his eyes.

'Don't you want to see the last veil drop?' she teased.

And his eyelids, disobeying him as though they were governed by some other being than their owner, popped open. It seemed the answer was yes.

The veil dropped.

And Max leapt in the chair like a deranged person.

She was so damned *hot*. The pale skin, the dark, lush hair. The tattoo—so bold, fiery, beautiful, sexy. So...*her*.

'Do you want me?'

'Yes,' he rasped.

'If you stop this time I'm going to kill you,' she said.

'If I stop I'll kill myself. Untie me, Cathy.'

'Not yet. I think I need to take one experience first.'

Max groaned, but was hardly in a position to argue.

The music had stopped. He wouldn't have heard it, anyway—his heart was banging like a timpani drum.

Then, very, very slowly, she glided over to him, adjusting her body with each step—front, side, back, side, front, arms up, down, out—letting him see every part of her body.

Finally, she was in front of him. She smiled, turned her back again, and her bottom was there—just *there*. If only his goddamned hands were free! She spread her legs, bent forward. And he could see the last hidden part of her: the hot, moist core. He whimpered like a baby—just couldn't help himself—and then with one sliding step backwards, one dip of her body, she snuggled onto his lap.

He let go with one moaning, keening cry of utter, delicious relief as her hands found him, as she moved to take him inside her. He thrust hard, blindly, and when she gasped and threw back her head he almost ripped his hands off, straining against the white silk that bound him.

And then incredibly, unbelievably, she was up again, and he was panting so hard he thought he might actually faint.

'Cut me loose,' Max ground out. 'No. Wait. While I still

have a shred of sanity go into the bathroom. Get a condom. Get ready to put it on me, Cathy—you'll have approximately five seconds before I fall on you like a madman.'

With a seductive little laugh she left him, steaming.

Catherine ran like a bullet to the bathroom, found the condoms, grabbed a handful, raced back to him.

Never mind Max falling on her like a madman—she wanted to fall on *him*. She was feral with need. Wanted to jam herself on him, sink her nails and teeth into him.

He had let her tie him up. He had let *her* be the one to control everything. He had given it all back to her—everything she'd lost. And now she wanted to take and take and take from him, until he couldn't think past the sight, the touch, the smell, the taste of her. *This* was what possession felt like. Like madness. She wanted to *own* him.

She moved behind him, dropped the condoms so she could work at the knots—but he'd struggled so hard against his bonds the knots were too tight.

'I need scissors,' she almost wailed.

'Bathroom,' he said, and she was off again, flying over the floor.

And then she was back, all but hacking the knots apart, and Max was free.

She grabbed the condoms from the floor and hurried around to the front of the chair, expecting him to surge up and grab her. For one moment it looked as though that was exactly what he would do—shirt half-on, pants around his ankles. He looked desperate enough to tackle her to the floor.

But as Catherine watched he closed his eyes and drew a deep, deep breath. Another. One more.

When he opened his eyes he looked grim and determined. He bent to remove his shoes. Then he kicked off his pants. His shirt came next.

'Works better if we're both naked,' he said as he stood.

And Catherine, drooling at the sight of his unfolding frame, had to agree.

He was magnificent. Long limbs. Lean muscle. Huge, straining erection. Holding himself so still and tense, as though scared to take a step.

And then he took that step. Just one. Stopped. His hands had fisted by his sides. The veins in his neck were standing out.

'So, Cathy,' he said, and his voice was unbelievably husky, 'can I touch you now?'

Catherine stared at him.

She could hear his breathing—harsh and laboured. See the fine trembling that was consuming him. Almost *feel* his heart pounding. He wanted her as desperately as she wanted him. And yet…he'd stopped.

He swallowed, waiting for her answer. Closed his eyes, gave his head a tiny shake. As if he was harnessing everything inside him, getting it under control.

*'Can I touch you now?'*

Five little words.

And she was tumbling, drowning, surging. In love.

Tears sprang to Catherine's eyes. 'Yes,' she whispered, and closed the space between them, winding her arms around his waist, holding on tightly despite the condoms clutched in one fist, her face against his chest. 'Yes, you can touch.' She slanted a look up at him, smiling tearily. 'And I can touch *you*, Max.'

As he looked down into her face, into her eyes, she could see he understood. As he always did. He took her face between his shaking hands and lowered his head to put his mouth on hers. Her heart was swelling, opening, breaking as his lips nudged hers, urging her to open her mouth *over* his, waiting for her to push his lips apart, to sweep her tongue inside. She explored his mouth with her tongue, pushing, thrusting, licking into him, exulting in her possession of this strong and wonderful man who was making it clear he was hers to do with as she wanted.

And she was going to take him, by God!

She grabbed his buttocks, yanking him in, squirming

against him to try and get closer, *closer*. And then his hands were simply everywhere. Her back, her hips, her bottom, her hair. As though he wanted to touch every part of her all at once.

And then, when her legs opened as though she needed him between them then, *right then*, he pulled back.

'Bed,' he said. 'Now.'

The next moment he was dragging her into the bedroom. He fell with her onto the bed, clutching her to his chest. Kissed *her* this time. Long and savage. Broke free, breathing hard.

'Condom,' he said. 'Give it to me. I'll be faster.'

'I want to do it,' Catherine said.

Max rolled onto his back, covering his face with his hands. 'Hurry, Cathy. At this rate I am going to last about twenty seconds.'

She ripped open the package, purred as she rolled the condom onto him. 'Twenty seconds is okay—for the first time.'

'We're down to ten seconds,' he said, and without further ado he flipped their positions and pushed inside her.

One, two, three, four strokes and he was coming, coming, *coming*—straining and ferocious.

He collapsed on top of her, his face buried against her neck, breathing hard still. 'Sorry, but you did say ten seconds would be okay for the first time,' he said, and then he started laughing.

'I agreed to twenty,' Catherine said—and then she started laughing too. 'Impatient,' she gasped out, 'as usual. And n-now you owe me ten seconds.'

Laughing. She laughed, laughed, *laughed*. So hard she snorted and her eyes streamed.

Max eased onto his elbows, looked down into her face. And the last piece of the puzzle clicked in his head. *This* last piece. Catherine-the-Great. With her glowing eyes and her passion-swollen mouth. Vibrant and furious and kind and fiery and smart and funny and brave and...*everything*.

Laughing. She was laughing. At last. Completely undone before him.

And she was his.

He was in love with her.

'I can do better than ten seconds,' he said around the sudden lump in his throat, and started moving purposefully down her body, leading with his mouth.

He reached her breasts, hovered there, looked up at her.

'One good thing about getting the edge taken off so fast is that now I get to play for a long, *long* time.'

And with that he took her nipple in his mouth and sucked.

Catherine groaned. 'Oh, God, Max.'

'*Oh, God*, is right,' he said, but this time he didn't look up, barely moved his mouth from her.

Max closed a hand gently around each breast, pressing them together so his tongue could move uninterrupted from one to the other and back, again and again, until Catherine was as weak and trembling as *he'd* been with his pathetic four-stroke effort. She was grabbing handfuls of his hair so hard it would have hurt if he hadn't been mindless with the erotic knowledge that her pebbled nipples were in his mouth.

She moved restlessly, whimpering, and he looked up at her, saw her licking her bottom lip. He wanted to lick that lip, too. He moved up her body, put his mouth on hers, slid his tongue inside her mouth—in, out, in, out, in, out. The same rhythm as her hips, which were thrusting against him.

'I'm ready for round two, Cathy,' he whispered to her, and she squirmed beneath him, opening her legs in wanton invitation.

'Me, too,' she said, all breathy and gorgeous.

Another long, drugging kiss. And then he said, 'But it's your turn,' and quickly rolled so that she was on top. 'Your turn to take me.'

She started to raise herself over him but he stopped her halfway, leaning up for another licking kiss of her mouth, one last sucking kiss for each nipple.

She wrenched a condom from where she'd scattered them

on the bed. As she tried to slide it onto him he squeezed her breasts, pinched her nipples, concentrating his intense focus there, wringing gasps and moans from her.

And then he looked down as she prepared to sheath him inside her and his hips jerked with need. But still he said, 'Wait—I want to touch you there first.'

Both his hands moved down, fingers easing into the slippery wetness.

'God, Cathy, how did I keep my hands off you for so long?'

She stayed, poised over him, letting his fingers dip and slide. He could feel her thighs trembling either side of him.

And then she said, 'I'm going to come, Max,' and she took him into her hands, guided him to her opening.

One of his hands moved to her tattooed hip; the other shifted so that his fingers could circle and pinch that small nub of nerves as she settled, hard, on him.

Almost immediately she was coming, moaning his name. But he kept going, stroking, touching with his fingers as he thrust up into her until he could feel her starting to tighten around him again.

'Cathy, you make me so hot and wild and crazy.'

She whimpered a response as she collapsed onto his chest, another orgasm ripping through her. But he couldn't hear what she said. His heart was roaring. He thrust again, groaning into her neck. Kept the rhythm up until he exploded.

With a shaking hand he stroked her hair. 'Get some rest, Cathy,' he whispered. 'Because tonight I'm going to make you come, and come, and come.'

That evening, as Catherine got ready for the all-important cocktail party, she thought of the almost surreal juxtaposition of today's ruthless professional discipline and last night's outrageous passion when Max had indeed made her come, and come, and come—to the point when she'd been half afraid to stand on her wobbly legs this morning.

Sitting next to Max, taking notes and conferring on various discussion points, she might have thought last night's debauchery was a scene from *Passion Flower*—except that every time Max had looked at her he'd smiled in a way she'd never seen him smile before, and she'd been able to tell he was remembering, too.

She checked herself in the mirror. Her make-up was dramatic and sexy. The red dress, wickedly low-cut, fitted her like a second skin and shimmered with spangles. She'd tumbled her hair onto her head in a soft, loose ballerina bun, with a tendril or two strategically placed to help hide the love-bite Max had planted on her neck, because make-up could only do so much. She'd vacillated between her old, musky perfume and her new lemon one—and ended up dabbing on a little of each.

The new and the old. Perfect.

She couldn't wait for Max to see her, smell her, taste her. The cocktail party would be like foreplay—each of them seeing the other gliding amongst the guests, knowing what was coming when the party was over.

The party was being held in a cordoned-off outdoor area close to the pool, with an emergency roof that could be extended in case of rain. She arrived early to check that everything was perfect—food and drinks ready to go, the low-key jazz band she'd hired in position, the flowers fresh and amazing. Marking time, waiting for the first sight of Max.

He arrived flanked by Darcy—who gave Catherine her own version of the death stare, complete with a show of teeth—and Doug.

One glinting smile from Max and Catherine's spirits surged. Even Darcy's proprietorial pawing of Max's arm couldn't affect her, because whatever happened tomorrow, next week, next month…tonight he was Catherine's.

And she was euphoric!

The euphoria lasted approximately twenty-five minutes.

Which was how long it took for RJ Harrow to arrive.

# CHAPTER THIRTEEN

CATHERINE SAW RJ'S EYES widen in appreciation as she came into his line of vision and her heart started hammering. He wasn't on the guest list. So how—why—was he here? And what was she going to do? Because she knew he would make his way to her.

And within ten minutes he had, ushered over by Eric.

'I hear you two know each other,' Eric said.

'Yes,' said Catherine, like death.

'How lucky that RJ happened to be in Australia on other business,' Eric said.

'You should have called me about Kurrangii, Cat,' RJ said to her, all *faux* reproach. 'You know Samawi Air is in investment mode, and this is right up our alley.'

She murmured something suitably vague as Eric scooted off to greet other arrivals.

Catherine made to follow Eric, but RJ grabbed her wrist. 'So, my little Cat landed on her feet.'

He leered like a villain in a melodrama, and Catherine— to her shock—giggled. And just like that the tension drained out of her. He didn't scare her, she realised. She was out of gaol and she was safe. Shock—and then euphoria rushed back.

'I detest being called Cat,' she said. 'And unless hell has frozen over...' She cocked her free hand around her ear. 'What's that? Hell *hasn't* frozen over? Well, then, not *your* Cat.'

RJ's eyes narrowed. 'We can fix that. For tonight at least.'

Catherine laughed. She couldn't help herself. With a disbelieving shake of her head she pulled on her hand, trying to break free—but he held it in a bruising grip.

'Not so fast,' he said, close to her ear. 'Unless you want me to tell Max all about our...*time*...together.'

She gave him a pitying smile. 'He knows all about our time together.'

His eyes narrowed. 'Told him, did you? But there are always two sides.'

'By all means tell him your side.'

'After,' he said, and started dragging her away from the area, smiling charmingly as he went.

Only her determination not to ruin Max's evening kept Catherine from screaming like a banshee as she was drawn inexorably along with him towards the pool, past the waterfall, into the darkness, until he had her shoved against the palm tree. *Max's* palm tree.

'Let me go or I'm going to scream,' she said, matter-of-factly.

'You won't do that. You never could bring yourself to spoil the party by screaming. You don't want to spoil *Max's* party, do you?'

'Actually,' Catherine said, still going with matter-of-fact, 'if the alternative is being slobbered over by you, Max will understand why I'm opting for the scream.'

She opened her mouth to let fly, but before she could make a sound RJ had wedged his mouth on hers, cutting off her breath. His mouth was bruising, wet. She could taste cigar.

She thought of Max seeing her like this. Vulnerable, defenceless, powerless. And the rage rushed at her. Her knee came up, forceful and sharp, into his groin. Fingers reached for his eyes.

A gasping squeal and she was free.

But she didn't run. Not this time. Not from *him*. She

scrubbed a hand across her mouth. 'You really need to learn how to kiss, RJ, because that was just pathetic.'

RJ had doubled over, clutching his groin with one hand, his face with the other.

Catherine heard the racing footsteps. Caught the scent. And then he was there. *Max*. She smiled tremulously at him. Wanting to laugh and cry. Simultaneously.

'Not the palm tree!' Max said, and got Catherine laughing. And, yes, crying. She just...*loved* him. So much.

And then Max looked at RJ.

'And if it isn't Dead Man Walking. Or should that be dead man hunching and squealing like a girl?' He inclined his head towards RJ's groin. 'Did you hit your mark this time, darling one?'

'Yes.'

'Excellent. Have you finished with him? Can I take over?' Max—perfectly conversational.

RJ tried to get a word out, but Max gave him an offhand, 'We're not talking to *you*,' and ignored him.

'What are you going to do?' Catherine asked.

'I can drown him for you, if you like.'

RJ blustered something about Catherine asking for it.

Max turned a look of such ferocity on him he quailed. 'Do you *want* to spend tonight looking for a dentist?' Max asked.

At that point RJ, looking terrified, pushed at Catherine—who went hurtling backwards towards the damned tree. Max lunged for her, and RJ made a run for freedom.

'Now, you see, that is *exactly* like Raymond,' Catherine complained as Max tugged her close and pulled a leaf out of her hair. 'Running away before I can finish.'

'Hang on—I'll get him for you,' Max said.

But when he turned to give chase it was to see a panic-stricken RJ so busily looking behind him that he barrelled into a poolside chair.

A loud splash later, and he and the chair were in the pool.

Max turned back to face Catherine. 'Do you really want me to get him? Or shall we just report him?'

Catherine moved back into Max's arms, rubbed her cheek against his chest. 'Will it stick?'

Max sighed. 'Who knows? But we have to do something.'

They were both aware of RJ wading out of the pool and hurrying away, but they ignored him.

'Okay—let's do it. And, regardless of the outcome, I'm going to get him where it hurts—Abu Najmah. I'm going to write an account of what he did to me and send it to the powers-that-be over there.'

Max nodded. 'And I'll do my bit and get the word out in my circles that he's not a fit and proper person to do business with. And then we'll put him in the past.' He held his arm out to her. 'You look beautiful, by the way. Red is your colour.'

'It's my favourite.'

'I know.'

'How?'

'The toenails that day. The peignoir that night. This dress. *You*.'

'You're very perceptive.'

'And you're wearing a new perfume. You smell even more divine than usual.'

'I call it "Phoenix".' Catherine took Max's arm. And then she laughed. 'Wow, I feel great!'

Catherine had slipped away from the party right after his speech, but Max knew she would be waiting for him in his cabin.

And there she was—out on the deck. The river. Soothing. She would have needed to be soothed after tonight's encounter. Because no matter how great she'd felt at that one moment, reaction was bound to have set in.

She turned, and he saw she'd been crying. His fiery, wonderful Cathy crying—he couldn't bear it.

She came slowly towards him, looking so soft and vulnerable he felt his whole body ache with the need to hold, to protect. Maybe he *did* have a Sir Galahad complex—but it was all directed at her. Just like the rest of him. All, *all*, for her.

A metre away from him she stopped, undid her dress. It dropped to the floor—*swoosh*—and she stood before him naked except for delicious red lace knickers.

'It really isn't about the way I look, is it?' she asked.

Max shook his head. 'I'd want you if you were wearing glasses, contact lenses, an eye-patch. Hair up, hair down, head shaved. In that red dress, or the peignoir, or the tweed skirt, or a sack…or nothing except your glorious phoenix rising from the ashes—the way *you* rose tonight.'

She smiled. 'Tonight I feel like I finally earned my ink. Thank you, Max.'

And then she walked into his arms.

'Thank you,' she said again, and then kissed him, her lips clinging, sweet as honey.

Outside, the rain hit. Drenching, soaking, sheeting down, ferocious—the way he felt about Catherine. The way he knew he would always feel about her. As if he was drowning in her, dying for her.

*Please love me. Please don't leave me. Please, please, please.*

He swung her into his arms and carried her to the bedroom. Laid her gently on the bed, let her lips cling to his… Until the sweetness was gone and the kiss had changed. Subsuming, devouring, possessive, wild. Lips seeking, teeth clashing, tongues shoving and tangling.

Max shifted so that he was looming over her. Dipped his head to kiss her again, *again*. Then dragged his mouth down her neck, over her breasts, pausing to lick and suck as Catherine used her hands in his hair to urge him on.

He edged down over her ribs, to her navel. A swirl of tongue, a kiss. And down, down… Over the red lace, breathing her in.

'Open,' he commanded, and her legs fell apart, and she was crying again as his mouth found her.

He kept kissing between her legs as his fingers gripped the lace at her hips, tugged it down. One tiny pause and his mouth was on her naked flesh, wet and hot, tongue stroking deeply into her. He shifted again, sucking the tiny nub of throbbing nerves into his mouth.

'Max!' she cried as she started to come, head thrown back on the pillow, moans ripping from her throat, fingers tangling in his hair. He kept the pressure steady and strong, over and over, until she was coming again and he thought he would die with the need to give her more, more, *more*.

'Please, Max,' she begged, and he slid up her body.

Max kissed her mouth, reaching blindly for the bedside table where they'd left the condoms. Kept kissing her as he ripped a condom free, slid it on, and then he was between Catherine's legs, his arms fully around her, holding her as close as his own flesh, wanting her closer still.

When at last he pushed within her Max's world stopped spinning. For one incredible, tight moment he held still, feeling only Catherine's hot, quivering core, seeing only her trembling eyelids as she waited for him to move inside her, hearing only the catch in her breath as she jerked her hips against his, urging him. And when he moved it was heaven. Stroking so fully, deeply, completely inside her. Silently chanting her name: *Cathy, Cathy, Cathy...*

'Thank you, thank you, thank you,' she said, as though she'd heard her name singing in his blood and was answering him. She wrapped her legs around him, pushing desperately against him.

When he felt her orgasm he let himself go with a harsh, gasping cry—blinding, almost unbearable. And then he collapsed, rolling to the side, dragging her with him. And then there were only harsh, shocked breaths, hands that couldn't stop touching, heartbeats that wouldn't slow.

'Thank you,' she said again.

But Max's throat was too tight to respond. Because he didn't want her thanks. He wanted her love.

Max wasn't sure what to expect when he opened his eyes the next morning.

But it wasn't to find Cathy gone.

She wasn't in the bed. Or the bathroom. The deck. Anywhere. He called her cabin—no answer. Her mobile—switched off.

His heart started to race for no apparent reason—because he knew she had to be somewhere. They weren't booked to fly home until Sunday. But he couldn't shake the feeling something was wrong.

He checked his watch. Riffled his hair. Blew out a breath. Tried her cabin again. Her mobile.

Without bothering to shower—because he *wanted* to reek of her, of sex with her—he pulled on pants and a T-shirt and hurried to the restaurant in case she'd opted for an early breakfast.

Not there.

He stopped at the reception desk. Very casual. Had they seen her?

One of the staff held out an envelope. Said something Max didn't hear because his brain had stopped functioning at the first sight of it. Because he knew. *Knew.*

Max returned to his cabin, carried the envelope onto the deck, looking to the river, which always soothed Cathy. But he wasn't soothed. Could barely think.

He saw something red on the wooden slats of the deck, glinting in the sun.

*Red.*

A spangle from Cathy's dress.

It brought him back to the moment. And he realised he had to know.

He tore open the envelope. One sheet of paper. A few short paragraphs.

*Dear Max*

*Please accept this letter as formal notification of my resignation from Rutherford Property.*

*While I have enjoyed my time at the company, personal circumstances have forced me to re-evaluate my career.*

*I thank you for your support during my time at the company, and wish Rutherford Property every success.*

*Thank you! Thank you so much.*
*Yours sincerely*
*Catherine North*

Even expecting it, Max felt as if he'd taken a blow to the chest.

*Personal circumstances...*

He picked up the red spangle, rubbed it between his fingers, stared at it. He looked down at the page again, let the words settle into his gut.

And felt the desperation claw at him—because she was leaving him.

But he loved her. How could she leave him when she was the last woman? *His* last woman? She was so *much* the last woman he might as well chop it off without her, because she'd ruined him for anyone else.

*Earth to Max—you never told her. How would she know?*

*Max to earth—she didn't* want *me to love her. She said love would make her pack up her desk.*

But she'd gone and packed up her desk, anyway. Which meant...who the hell knew?

His hand closed hard over the sparkle of red.

His temper flared.

Well, sorry, *no*! In fact, ditch the sorry. Just no.

If she thought, after putting him through that week of torture, she was going to flit off into the sunset without leaving him *any* of her, she was sorely mistaken.

Never to see her again—when he needed her. Needed her *everywhere*.

He opened his fist, looked at the tiny glinting piece of red. All he had of her.

No. Not happening. *Not*.

His heart gave an approving thump as that thought settled.

He was experienced with women. Successful in business. A shrewd entrepreneur, used to getting his own way. A natural and efficient problem-solver.

She might be Catherine-the-Great—all right she *was* Catherine-the-Great—but she was not going to get the better of him.

It was time to take control.

Time to make her see she belonged with him. And if she didn't love him, he'd make her!

She'd written a damned book about him, hadn't she? Jennifer loved Alex. She was Jennifer. He was Alex. So she could damned well write herself into loving him. Hell, he'd write it *for* her!

Because she was his. His. *His.*

'His': *that* was the word of the day. Of the week, of the year. His, forever.

# CHAPTER FOURTEEN

CATHY SPENT A miserable weekend with her thoughts.

Her accusing, guilty thoughts.

It had hit her, right about the time when Max had made his speech at the cocktail party, that he was perfect—a defender, a protector, honourable and caring, generous and funny and gorgeous…and just damned *perfect*.

And that she, by contrast, was the female equivalent of RJ Harrow. Because she had forced herself on Max against his will!

And as if that wasn't perfidious enough, when she'd worn him down, and he'd helped her petals unfurl to the point when they were doing a victory dance across the garden bed, she'd refused to do the one thing he'd asked of her: stay.

But how could she stay when she loved him so? He didn't want her to love him. He'd warned her *not* to love him. Surely he wouldn't want her to stay when she'd gone ahead and done it, anyway?

Deep, deep in her black heart she'd thought—*hoped*?— Max would be so furious with her for leaving he'd demand to see her in the office on Monday morning. But despite a few missed calls from him while she was in-flight he'd left no messages, and there had been no calls since.

He'd just let her go.

Let her go. Like it was no big deal. Because he didn't love her. He would never make her the 'last woman' because she wasn't his type. And she was damned sure she wasn't the type to stand by and watch him move on to someone else when their affair ended.

Man, this unrequited love business sucked.

Monday morning dawned and Catherine woke depressed. Two Mondays ago she would have been getting ready for work. Today she was jobless, with nothing to do except write *Passion Flower*. And she just didn't have the heart to string together a new fantasy. Because she couldn't improve on the reality she'd had with Max.

So maybe she would just...well, connect with him without his knowledge. Via her Rutherford Property email. Or at least see if her access had been cut off—as it *should* have been if someone was doing their job properly.

Deep breath.

Okay.

Opening emails *now*.

And it was there. A message from Max. And *bang* went her heart. Bang, bang, bang, bang.

She stared at the subject line: NEED HELP. Of *course* it would be in capital letters—typical Max! And then, sucking in a big brave breath, she opened it.

Oh.

It was...work! Work? *Work*.

Oh.

A list of questions about Kurrangii—of all the ironies—with a file attached. Well, she supposed answering his questions was the least she could do after resigning so precipitately and leaving him in the lurch.

It took four hours.

Tuesday morning there came a file on the Canada project, and a list of questions was waiting in her inbox. She answered and—four hours and thirty minutes later—sent it back.

Wednesday it was the Brazil eco resort—HELP! I'M DROWNING in the subject line. List of questions.

Five hours.

Thursday—another Kurrangii file.

Five hours.

Friday: WHAT AM I GOING TO DO? with assorted questions concerning office administration. Including a query about her—her *job description*?

Whoa! Like...*whoa*!

How *dared* he involve her in finding her own replacement when he hadn't even had the decency to mention her own resignation? The only way she was going to help was if he was looking for a ninety-year-old woman or a straight man or a lesbian. Someone she wouldn't need to chainsaw in half.

Furious, she emailed back: Mr Rutherford, I resigned.

Thirty seconds later, back came the reply.

I didn't accept that. You've had enough sulking time, so man up, Phoenix Firebrand. See you Monday.

Man up? Phoenix Firebrand? Sulking time? *Sulking?*

Catherine-the-Great did not *sulk*.

On Monday morning, after a weekend of uncontained wrath that had seen the tinkling demise of an array of glassware and ceramics, Catherine got out of bed, dressed, and went to work.

She was going to *make* Max Rutherford love her.

'Love': word of the day. And skip the 'unrequited'.

# CHAPTER FIFTEEN

CATHERINE WAS WEARING a snug summer-weight skirt suit in eye-popping red. Her hair was in a loose bun at her nape and she was wearing new glasses—heavy, black, rectangular frames. *Very* sexy librarian.

At her desk. Waiting for Max. Ready to make him beg for mercy!

Max checked for a moment as he came around the corner from the lift lobby and saw her. Said 'Huh.' Then walked on.

He paused at her desk. 'Morning, Cathy.'

'Good morning, Max.'

Then he disappeared into his office and the day passed normally—like any day in the office pre–mad sexual escapade.

Which was *infuriating*.

This was work—okay, she got it. She *wanted* work to proceed as usual. But were they not going to reference what had happened in Queensland *at all*?

Well, if nothing happened by six o'clock she was going into Max's office to chase him around his desk.

At three o'clock in the afternoon Max poked his head out. 'Cathy, can you collect a courier package from Reception? Straight away. I think it's urgent.' And he disappeared back into his office.

Ooooh, he was pushing it!

But Catherine dutifully went downstairs and got the

package—which was addressed to her, anyway, so Max could shove his 'urgent' where the sun didn't shine.

She sat at her desk, opened the package. Extracted a sheaf of pages.

*Phoenix Firebrand—a Passion Flower book* was printed in big bold type across the top of first page.

*Ooohhhhhhhh...*

*Alex sat in Jennifer's chair, eyes glued to her computer screen. The words were there, but he couldn't quite take them in. Couldn't quite take it in, even though the resemblance was staring him in the face.*

*He was Max Rutherford?*

*The woman he was in love with had written him into a steamy romance novel?*

*Did it mean...could it mean...she was in love with him, too?*

Catherine laughed, then clapped a hand over her mouth. Crazy. This was crazy. *She* was crazy. Because this could not be happening.

She kept reading, her heart racing... Reading, reading...

And then it was there—today's scene—and the tears started.

*Alex saw her sitting in her usual chair and his heart sang.*

*Jennifer was exactly where she belonged. With him.*

*If he were an eloquent guy he could tell her what she meant to him.*

*He could tell her that his enjoyment of anything equestrian was a thing of the past.*

Laugh. Oh, God, how could she *not* laugh at that?

*He could tell her she was it for him. His life, his world, his aching love. He didn't care that she was a*

*maniac, because he was, too. He didn't care how often
she gave him the death stare—as long as she did it.
He didn't care about anything, except...her. Being his.
His last woman. The one.*

She heard a sound. Looked up to find Max watching her
from his office doorway.

'What do you think?' he asked.

'Don't give up your day job,' Catherine said, wiping her
eyes.

He smiled. 'I won't if you don't. Although it was easy
to write, Cathy. I guess it's always simple when you think
you're going to die. And I think I *will* die if I can't have you.'
Laugh. 'No pressure, though.'

'Oh, no pressure?' she asked. 'Because it feels like pressure.'

'Okay, pressure,' Max conceded with an easy shrug. 'So?
Catherine-the-Great can't take a little pressure?'

Catherine kept her eyes on him as she stood, walked over
to him, gazed up at him. 'Catherine-the-Great can take anything you dish out.'

He touched her cheek—just as Nell came barrelling
around the corner.

Nell stopped, turned tail—as any sane person would
when confronted with that annihilating glare—and ran for
the elevator.

'I'm going to kill the next person who walks onto this
floor,' Max said.

'Chainsaw,' Catherine offered.

'Huh?'

'Chainsaw—it's my preferred murder weapon—not that
Nell is a tall leggy blonde. And, really, she is so smart and
funny and great. She sings, you know?'

Max stared at Catherine for a long, delighted moment,
and then he laughed. 'No, I didn't know she sang, but I'm
glad you're sparing her the chainsaw.'

'Now, you see? How could I *not* love you? Even the chain-saw doesn't scare you.'

Max's slow lopsided smile flashed. Stayed. 'Didn't quite catch that,' he said.

'I love you. So much.'

'Okay, in that case you get this...thing...' Reaching into his pocket, he extracted a small jewellery box. 'It's for the good of humankind that we get married, you know. Because we can't have you chainsawing stray blondes and me ripping the heads off any man you touch.'

He opened the box and *wrenched* a ring out. Typical Max!

'Whew...' He breathed out. 'I'm kind of nervous. I've never done this before.'

'And you won't be doing it again, so get it right, Max.'

'I'm not getting on my knee, Cathy, if that's what you mean.'

'I'll be happy if you can just get that ring on my finger with breaking a bone in the rush.'

'It's a ruby,' he said, taking her hand in his. 'Your colour, Firebrand.'

'Huh,' she said as he slid the ring onto her finger.

'Huh? What's with the *huh*?'

She smiled up at him. 'You're asking me? Well, in this instance it means please kiss me. What does it mean when *you* say it every other minute?'

He smiled back at her, raised her hand, kissed the palm, the back, the finger where his ring sat perfectly.

'It means...I long for you,' he said.

And then he took her in his arms, hugging her so hard she feared for the structural purity of her ribcage. Kissed her—a long, lush claim of a kiss.

He gave her his slow, lopsided smile as he released her. 'Thank God you're back, because I was dreading the prospect of having to find another personal assistant.'

'Is that the best you've got?' Catherine asked, narrowing her eyes at him. 'That you want to marry me to spare you having to recruit another plain-Jane personal assistant?'

'*Another* one? Who was the first? Not you—that's for sure.' He kissed her again. 'Not that I mind if you want to chase me around the desk,' he said. 'But I don't think that's going to provide much sport for either of us. I'll be very easy to catch. I've wanted you to catch me since your second week on the job—your first ever volcanic eruption, about a Canadian staffing issue, as I recall.'

'I don't erupt.'

'Oh, you *so* do! So it's good thing you ended up with a boss who likes the occasional hot lava flow. Speaking of which—I've got some ideas that will be very good for your career, too.'

Catherine stiffened and pulled out of his arms, but before she could retreat more than a step Max grabbed both her hands to keep her there. 'Not *this* career, obviously,' he clarified, 'because you've already got *that* sewn up. Sleeping with the boss.'

'*What?*'

'Hey, it's not so bad—I'm sleeping with mine, too. You know—partners. Which I guess means I'm not sleeping with my personal assistant. Hmm... I'm not sure that won't re-ignite my father complex. Maybe I *should* get a new personal assistant.'

'Chainsaw.'

He laughed. 'Well, anyway, my ideas concern your career as a romance novelist.'

'And how do you figure you can help me with that?'

'Well, I'm Alex Taylor, and I'm going to let you prop me up around the office—or anywhere, really—for research purposes. Try out the positions. You know—the sex scenes. Because, to be honest, *Passion Flower* needs more sex.'

'Oh, it does, does it?'

'Well, *better* sex, at any rate. Because Alex... Meh! *Wimp!* Now, I have some ideas...'

'Oh, *do* you?'

He pulled her in. 'Starting with that scene in Alex's office. The bit about the hairpins scattering...' He dipped his head, kissed her until she was breathless. Smiled into her eyes as his fingers slid into her hair. 'I want to try it. Right now. And you'll see what I mean.'

\* \* \* \* \*

# *Mills & Boon® Hardback*

## *October 2014*

# ROMANCE

# MEDICAL

*Mills & Boon® Large Print*

*October 2014*

# ROMANCE

| | |
|---|---|
| Ravelli's Defiant Bride | Lynne Graham |
| When Da Silva Breaks the Rules | Abby Green |
| The Heartbreaker Prince | Kim Lawrence |
| The Man She Can't Forget | Maggie Cox |
| A Question of Honour | Kate Walker |
| What the Greek Can't Resist | Maya Blake |
| An Heir to Bind Them | Dani Collins |
| Becoming the Prince's Wife | Rebecca Winters |
| Nine Months to Change His Life | Marion Lennox |
| Taming Her Italian Boss | Fiona Harper |
| Summer with the Millionaire | Jessica Gilmore |

# HISTORICAL

| | |
|---|---|
| Scars of Betrayal | Sophia James |
| Scandal's Virgin | Louise Allen |
| An Ideal Companion | Anne Ashley |
| Surrender to the Viking | Joanna Fulford |
| No Place for an Angel | Gail Whitiker |

# MEDICAL

| | |
|---|---|
| 200 Harley Street: Surgeon in a Tux | Carol Marinelli |
| 200 Harley Street: Girl from the Red Carpet | Scarlet Wilson |
| Flirting with the Socialite Doc | Melanie Milburne |
| His Diamond Like No Other | Lucy Clark |
| The Last Temptation of Dr Dalton | Robin Gianna |
| Resisting Her Rebel Hero | Lucy Ryder |

# *Mills & Boon® Hardback*
## *November 2014*

# ROMANCE

| | |
|---|---|
| **A Virgin for His Prize** | Lucy Monroe |
| **The Valquez Seduction** | Melanie Milburne |
| **Protecting the Desert Princess** | Carol Marinelli |
| **One Night with Morelli** | Kim Lawrence |
| **To Defy a Sheikh** | Maisey Yates |
| **The Russian's Acquisition** | Dani Collins |
| **The True King of Dahaar** | Tara Pammi |
| **Rebel's Bargain** | Annie West |
| **The Million-Dollar Question** | Kimberly Lang |
| **Enemies with Benefits** | Louisa George |
| **Man vs. Socialite** | Charlotte Phillips |
| **Fired by Her Fling** | Christy McKellen |
| **The Twelve Dates of Christmas** | Susan Meier |
| **At the Chateau for Christmas** | Rebecca Winters |
| **A Very Special Holiday Gift** | Barbara Hannay |
| **A New Year Marriage Proposal** | Kate Hardy |
| **A Little Christmas Magic** | Alison Roberts |
| **Christmas with the Maverick Millionaire** | Scarlet Wilson |

# MEDICAL

| | |
|---|---|
| **Playing the Playboy's Sweetheart** | Carol Marinelli |
| **Unwrapping Her Italian Doc** | Carol Marinelli |
| **A Doctor by Day...** | Emily Forbes |
| **Tamed by the Renegade** | Emily Forbes |

# ROMANCE

| | |
|---|---|
| Christakis's Rebellious Wife | Lynne Graham |
| At No Man's Command | Melanie Milburne |
| Carrying the Sheikh's Heir | Lynn Raye Harris |
| Bound by the Italian's Contract | Janette Kenny |
| Dante's Unexpected Legacy | Catherine George |
| A Deal with Demakis | Tara Pammi |
| The Ultimate Playboy | Maya Blake |
| Her Irresistible Protector | Michelle Douglas |
| The Maverick Millionaire | Alison Roberts |
| The Return of the Rebel | Jennifer Faye |
| The Tycoon and the Wedding Planner | Kandy Shepherd |

# HISTORICAL

| | |
|---|---|
| A Lady of Notoriety | Diane Gaston |
| The Scarlet Gown | Sarah Mallory |
| Safe in the Earl's Arms | Liz Tyner |
| Betrayed, Betrothed and Bedded | Juliet Landon |
| Castle of the Wolf | Margaret Moore |

# MEDICAL

| | |
|---|---|
| 200 Harley Street: The Proud Italian | Alison Roberts |
| 200 Harley Street: American Surgeon in London | Lynne Marshall |
| A Mother's Secret | Scarlet Wilson |
| Return of Dr Maguire | Judy Campbell |
| Saving His Little Miracle | Jennifer Taylor |
| Heatherdale's Shy Nurse | Abigail Gordon |

# MILLS & BOON®

## Why shop at millsandboon.co.uk?

Each year, thousands of romance readers find their perfect read at millsandboon.co.uk. That's because we're passionate about bringing you the very best romantic fiction. Here are some of the advantages of shopping at www.millsandboon.co.uk:

* **Get new books first**—you'll be able to buy your favourite books one month before they hit the shops

* **Get exclusive discounts**—you'll also be able to buy our specially created monthly collections, with up to 50% off the RRP

* **Find your favourite authors**—latest news, interviews  and new releases for all your favourite authors and series on our website, plus ideas for what to try next

* **Join in**—once you've bought your favourite books, don't forget to register with us to rate, review and join in the discussions

Visit **www.millsandboon.co.uk**
for all this and more today!